THE BROODING FRENCHMAN'S PROPOSAL

0132375542

THE BROODING FRENCHMAN'S PROPOSAL

BY

REBECCA WINTERS

First published in Great Britain 2009
Large Print edition 2009
Harlequin Mills & Boon Limited,
Eton House, 18-24 Paradise Road,
Richmond, Surrey TW9 1SR

ISBN: 978 0 263 20638 8

Set in Times Roman 16¾ on 20¼ pt.
16-1109-45792

Harlequin Mills & Boon policy is to use papers that are natural, renewable and recyclable products and made from wood grown in sustainable forests. The logging and manufacturing process conform to the legal environmental regulations of the country of origin.

Printed and bound in Great Britain
by CPI Antony Rowe, Chippenham, Wiltshire

To all you wonderful readers who've been so faithful
and have sent words of kindness and appreciation
through your letters and e-mails.
Every author should be so lucky.

CHAPTER ONE

TOWARD evening, Laura Aldridge, dressed in a cocktail dress of apricot-colored chiffon, stepped out onto the balcony of her bedroom at the Laroche villa. It overlooked the shimmering blue Mediterranean, and down a few steps lay a crescent-shaped swimming pool to complete the magical setting.

Located on Cap Ferrat, a small peninsula on the French Riviera, the villa, heavily guarded with security, formed part of the treasured real estate of the European aristocracy.

The balmy air of early July felt like the tropics. She lifted her fine-boned face to the gentle breeze filled with the scent of roses. It teased the ends of her pale-gold hair and caused the chiffon to flutter against her generously proportioned figure.

For the first time in six months Laura could breathe more easily knowing Ted didn't have a clue where she was. The men he'd hired to keep tabs on her, his way of reminding her she was his possession and he was going to get her back, wouldn't have been able to trace the helicopter that had whisked her here earlier today. To elude him for a few hours, let alone a day and a night, was so liberating she wished she could disappear from his radar forever.

Since her legal separation from Ted Stillman, Laura had been going by her maiden name of Aldridge while she fought for the divorce he'd vowed never to give her. He wasn't about to let her spoil his run for congress next year. By threatening to use the millions of dollars from his high-profile, politically ambitious family to keep their case tangled up in the courts, he hoped to bring her to her senses.

It would be to his detriment though, because

she refused to go back to him and had no desire to ever get married again. She'd removed her rings. All she cared about now was never having to see him again. Being thousands of miles away from the Stillman political machine helped. Saint-Jean-Cap-Ferrat was the playground of princes, and not even Ted's family with all their influence and connections had an entrée to it—thank heaven.

By a stroke of fate she was the guest of Guy Laroche and his wife, Chantelle, whom she'd met eleven years earlier in California. The summer before starting college Laura had been a part-time lifeguard and babysitter at the five-star Manhattan Beach Resort Hotel catering to VIPs from all over the world. Her boss had assigned her to baby sit the Laroche child, impressing upon her that the Laroche name moved mountains in the financial world of the Côte d'Azur.

They'd brought their one-year-old son Paul with them, a little boy Laura absolutely adored. Over that ten-day period he went from clinging to chairs and tables, to taking a few steps on his own toward her. His endearing ways caught at her heart. And she had often dreamed that one day she would have a darling, dark-haired boy of her own just like him.

When the three of them had flown on to Hawaii, Laura had felt a wrench to see them go. In that short time Chantelle had almost become like an older sister to her, and Guy had been the most charming man Laura had ever met. The French couple had been so in love and so crazy about Paul, it had been a joy to get to know them.

They'd all become such good friends, and the Laroches had made Laura promise that if she were ever to travel to France, she could stay with them for as long as she wanted. In the beginning they had sent her postcards from all their travels and pictures of Paul from Cap Ferrat where they lived, but in time they lost touch.

It wasn't until two days ago, while Laura was on a work assignment in Siena, Italy, for the Palio horse race, that she heard some tourists speaking French and remembered the French couple and their baby. Though she'd be flying home from Rome shortly, she decided to phone the Laroche company and see if she could reach them just to say hello.

When Guy had realized who was calling, he sounded overjoyed to hear from her. By an amazing coincidence he and Paul were joining old friends in Siena to watch the Palio, something they did every year, and Guy had insisted on meeting up with Laura there. She would sit at his table for dinner while they got reacquainted.

Laura wondered why he didn't mention Chantelle coming with him, but since he didn't offer an explanation, she didn't ask.

Late yesterday afternoon she'd had her reunion with Guy and little Paul, who was now twelve and as handsome as she'd imagined. Though it was a heartwarming moment, she sensed right away that something was wrong.

Guy had changed from the fun-loving man she remembered into someone who looked older than his forty-four years. His dark-brown hair had traces of silver and his patrician features were more pronounced. He'd become so serious. Paul, too, seemed too sober and polite for a boy his age.

After seating Laura at his right, Guy made all the introductions, starting with his good friend Maurice Charrière and his wife Yvette. They'd brought their son Remy who was good friends with Paul. Once Laura had met everyone they began eating, but at one point Guy started to choke on his food.

Since Laura was sitting next to him, she didn't notice his distress at first. Neither did the party of intelligent, well-dressed people with him. When he tried to stand up, it became clear he was struggling. They all looked horrified and got to their feet, but no one knew exactly how to help him.

Being a part-time CPR instructor and life-guard for over a decade, Laura immediately acted on instinct and jumped up from her chair to get his breathing passage cleared. Though she'd saved many lives from near drownings—including her husband Ted's—this was her first save on land with the Heimlich maneuver.

As soon as Guy had recovered enough to be comfortable again, he was embarrassingly grateful. In his beautiful English he thanked her profusely and made a huge fuss over her for saving his life. Laura assured him that anyone who had knowledge of the Heimlich could have done it and she'd just happened to be in the right spot at the right time. Everyone disagreed and Maurice claimed her to be a heroine.

Later that evening, after the riders had galloped by in all their fabulous trappings, Guy accompanied her to her hotel while Paul stayed behind with Remy and his parents. Before she went up to her room Guy begged her to change her flight until the day after and come to the villa in Cap Ferrat the next day. Chantelle wanted to see her.

Over dinner Guy had informed Laura that

Chantelle had been hurt in a car accident three months ago. Though no bones had been broken, she'd been severely bruised on her legs. Now she was physically recovered and could walk the way she did before. However, she clung to her wheelchair like it was a security blanket and refused to get out of it and resume her life again.

Laura cringed to hear the awful news. It explained the dramatic change in him.

According to Guy, the psychological impairment had made her paranoid, unwilling to be with people, but Chantelle had insisted that he bring Laura home with him. Since Laura had finished her work and was ready to fly back to Los Angeles, she didn't have a reason why she couldn't accept their invitation. In the end she said she could put off her flight to the States for a day and then fly out on the next flight from nearby Nice.

The following morning Guy had her flown to Cap Ferrat in his helicopter. It landed on his property where a limo drove her the short distance to the entrance of his Mediterranean-style villa. She walked into a world of art treasures, murals, mirrors, Persian rugs and sumptuously appointed rooms decorated in silks and damasks. The classic furnishings mixed with some contemporary pieces made it a show-place and a haven.

After one of the maids had shown her to a dreamy guest suite of pale pink and cream where she'd be staying the night, Guy came for her and took her to see Chantelle who, at the age of forty-three, still looked like she could grace the cover of *Vogue* magazine in her stunning black-and-white cocktail dress.

When Laura had first met her in California, she'd thought Guy's beautiful brunette wife had that Audrey Hepburn look…small, graceful. But the thing that struck Laura now was the lack of vivaciousness that had been an integral part of her personality eleven years ago. Her sad brown eyes seemed to carry the grief of the world in them.

She seemed truly happy to see Laura again,

and when Guy had told her about his choking experience, Chantelle had thanked her for saving her husband's life. She had told Laura that she wanted her to stay at their home for as long as she could, but no demonstrative hugs accompanied her offer. She certainly wasn't the gregarious person she used to be.

It was so unlike the old Chantelle that Laura wanted to cry her eyes out. Only now did she realize how difficult this change in his formerly, outgoing, loving wife must be for Guy. She could understand why he and Paul were so subdued. According to them, Chantelle had become paralyzed with fear since the accident.

Laura was acquainted with fear and knew that it came in many forms. In the beginning of her marriage, she'd learned things about Ted that had caused her to fall out of love with him. However, fear of reprisal had prevented her from confronting him, let alone standing up to the powerful Stillman dynasty. If she'd had more courage, she would have left Ted within months of the ceremony.

Obviously Chantelle was suffering from a different kind of fear. The experience of being trapped in her car for four hours before someone had found her had scarred her psyche in some complicated way. Laura carried her own psychological scars and couldn't blame Chantelle for hers, but she understood Guy's anguish.

Laura thought back to the friendship she'd maintained with one of the people she'd once saved from drowning. The teenager was in his twenties now, but he was still terrified of the water. She suspected Chantelle refused to get out of the wheelchair because she was terrified people would think she was ready to resume life. But as Laura had discovered, you couldn't make a move until your mind gave you permission.

In sympathy with the Laroches' tragic situation, she left the veranda and went back in the room to put on some lotion before joining the party. While she was applying it, she heard a rap on the door to her luxurious suite.

She guessed it was one of the maids, but when she opened it she discovered Guy standing there, looking distinguished in a sport shirt and slacks in a linen color. Though he appeared too drawn and worried for someone in his prime, the rest of his body seemed fit enough and tanned.

"Do you mind if we talk for a minute?"

"You mean here?'

"Yes. I'd rather no one else overheard us."

"If that's what you wish. Please, come in."

The foyer led into a sitting room with a spacious bedroom and bathroom hidden beyond the French doors. He sat down on one of the upholstered Louis XV chairs. She took a seat on the Jacquard-print love seat facing him.

Leaning forward with his elbows resting on his knees he said, "Before you meet everyone, I was hoping we could talk seriously for a moment. Would your husband be disappointed if you didn't get back to California right away? I'm asking for a specific reason."

Up to now Laura had avoided talking about her past, but Guy seemed so intent she didn't hold back. "I've been legally separated from my husband for six months, Guy," she admitted. "My divorce can't come soon enough."

Lines bracketed his mouth. "I'm sorry you're in so much pain. I had no idea."

His compassion prompted her to tell him the truth. "Any pain I suffered happened during my two-year marriage, which turned out to be a profound mistake. I assure you the separation has been the cure. My husband is fighting the divorce and keeping tabs on me, hoping to get me to come back to him, but it won't happen. I plan to win my divorce in my next court appearance."

She could hear his mind working. "Forgive me for speaking frankly then, but is there someone else waiting for your return?"

"No," she answered quietly. Even if there were someone, her attorney had told her to stay clear of any man so Ted couldn't use it for fuel against her.

"What's wrong with the men in your country?"

"Not the men, Guy. Me. I made an error in judgment when I married my husband. Since the separation I've been too busy traveling with my job to think about anything or anyone else. Why do you want to know?"

A sigh escaped his lips. "You've met Françoise of course."

Laura nodded. She was the middle-aged woman who helped out with Paul and provided companionship for Chantelle during the day while Guy was at work.

"She's going on vacation for two weeks starting tomorrow. I've scheduled another woman to fill in, but I was hoping I could influence you to stay on while Françoise is gone, provided your work schedule could allow it."

"Guy—"

"Let me finish," he implored. "When

Chantelle said you were welcome to stay and for as long as you wanted, I was overjoyed. Since the accident she hasn't shown an interest in anyone. But she trusts you. After the way you took care of Paul in California, she loved you. Since you two have a history together, it's obvious she doesn't feel like you'll ask more of her than she's willing to give."

The man was desperate.

"Much as I'd like to be of help, I'm not a doctor."

He shook his head. "She already has the best there is. I'm talking about her response to you. If you were to be around during the day, not every minute of course, I'm hoping that one of these mornings soon she'll start to confide in you like she once did. It's my opinion you could find a way to help her open up. I'd give everything I had for such a miracle."

Laura grew restless. "Today she responded to me, but you know as well as I do a short visit is a good one. I'm afraid that if I stayed, she'd grow to resent me being around and close up completely. I wouldn't want you to take the risk of that happening."

"There'd be no risk. You're a very peaceful person, and just what she needs. You handled Paul so beautifully she accepted you without question eleven years ago. That hasn't changed. It's why I feel you could be of help. If you would extend your time here a little longer, who knows what could happen."

"I don't know, Guy."

"Just promise me you'll think about it," he begged. "Naturally I would pay you a generous salary."

Laura drew in a sharp breath. "I'm flattered to think you feel my presence could benefit her, but I would never take your money." Laura managed just fine on the money she made earning her living, and she hated the idea of receiving money she hadn't earned herself through hard work, even if she were entitled to it. She hadn't touched the money the court had ordered Ted to pay her and was thinking of donating it to a charity.

Laura's experience with Ted had made her wary of men with a lot of money and power. Too late she realized Ted had chosen her to be his trophy wife, not the love of his life. Like all the Stillman men, he had thought nothing of being with other women while hiding behind his marriage to Laura, but it appeared that Guy, who could buy the Stillmans' assets many times over, wasn't cut from the same kind of cloth.

"Does that mean you would consider staying here out of friendship then?" His eyes went suspiciously bright. "I might have died at dinner from lack of oxygen if you hadn't acted as fast as you did. I feel closer to you now than ever. That's why I'm going to tell you something very personal.

"Chantelle and I have both been given a second chance at life, a life she used to embrace, but since the accident things have changed. We have drifted apart and I feel a gaping hole opening between us. In the past we always attended the Palio with the Charrières. This year she told me to go without her. I only went with

Paul because she got agitated when I told her I wouldn't leave her.

"Something is terribly wrong and holding her back. The psychiatrist working with her is frustrated there has been no breakthrough yet. She hasn't allowed me to make love to her since the accident. I love my wife, Laura. I'm willing to do anything to get her past that barrier she has erected, but I'm afraid something happened while she was waiting to be rescued that terrified her."

"Like what?"

"Maybe some monster came along and molested her while she was trapped and she can't bring herself to tell me."

Laura shuddered at the thought. She had to agree it was possible, though she couldn't imagine it. "You don't think she would have told you?"

He jumped up from the chair. "I don't know. I don't know anything anymore." Guy was in pain. The way his voice throbbed revealed his agony.

Chantelle Laroche had to be one of the

luckiest women alive to be truly loved by her husband. Not just on the surface, but deep down in his heart and soul where it counted.

She supposed Carl, her boss in L.A., might be willing to let her extend her time in Europe for another two weeks and call it her vacation. She could even make it a working holiday, which she knew would please him. She doubted she could make a real difference with Chantelle, though if Guy was this determined to get his wife back, Laura was willing to try to get on her old footing with Chantelle.

"Tell you what, Guy. My boss should be in his office right now. I'll phone him and if he says it's all right, I'll be happy to stay and see what I can do. Chantelle was so wonderful to me back then, and who wouldn't adore it here with all this beauty? You live in a paradise only a few people in the world are privileged to see."

The men Ted had hired to follow her every move would have to possess extra powers to know her location right now. Two weeks free of the Stillman net would be a bonus she hadn't counted on this trip to Europe. In her heart of hearts she had to admit that in wanting to keep her whereabouts a secret from Ted, Guy's proposal couldn't have come at a better time.

He moved closer to grasp her hands. "You are an angelic woman, Laura. I don't know what good I've done in this life for you to come into it again at the moment you did, but I will always be indebted to you. Whatever you need or want, it's yours."

"Thank you." She rose to her feet and accompanied him to the door. "I'll join you after I've made my phone call."

"I can't ask for more than that."

Raoul Laroche slipped into his brother's villa through a side entrance closest to his own smaller villa on the south of the family's private estate. He joined Maurice who stood just inside the French doors of the living room. *"Eh bien, Maurice. Qu'est-ce qui se passe?"*

His head turned. "*Bonsoir,* Raoul! I didn't know you were back from Switzerland already."

"I finished business faster than I thought and got home this afternoon," he muttered. "As Guy was leaving the office he told me he was giving a party, but he didn't tell me why. What's the occasion? Since the accident Chantelle has avoided company like the plague."

"This is different. He wanted everyone to meet Mrs. Aldridge, the American woman you're staring at."

Raoul realized he *was* staring. It irritated him that Maurice had noticed. "Who is she?"

"The woman who saved him from choking to death."

His black brows met. "Literally?"

After Chantelle's accident, the idea that his elder brother had experienced a close call like that wasn't exactly the best news in what had started out to be a hellish afternoon. He'd received another abusive phone call from his ex-wife, Danielle, swearing she would end her life if he didn't give their marriage another chance. Raoul had become weary of her attention-seeking tactics and had cut her off, but the distaste he had felt stayed with him.

"Quite literally." Maurice sounded shaken.

"When was this?"

"Last evening at the Palio in Siena. We were eating dinner with Luigi before the race started. I didn't realize Guy was even in trouble until she came flying to the rescue. She grabbed him and performed the Heimlich maneuver. Out came a piece of roll lodged in his throat and suddenly he could breathe again. It was over within minutes."

Raoul murmured *Grace à Dieu.* He was thankful his brother was all right, but continued to frown. Guy hadn't said anything to him about the incident while they had both been in the office earlier, and it was strange for him not to share something that had been a life-and-death situation. "What she's doing here in Cap Ferrat?"

"Guy wanted to do something to thank her

and decided a party would be a good way to celebrate."

"And Chantelle agreed?" Considering the guilt Guy had suffered over feeling responsible for Chantelle's present condition, not to mention the fragile state of their marriage at this point, this piece of information was somewhat disturbing. The woman was a virtual stranger, even if she had saved him from choking.

"It would seem so. Mrs. Aldridge is extraordinary," Maurice exclaimed. The awe in his eyes and voice as his gaze wandered over her left little to the imagination. This woman might be at least fifteen years younger, but age didn't matter when she was built like a mermaid decorating the prow of an eighteenth-century ship.

Even from the distance separating them, she oozed more unconscious sensuality than should be let loose on humanity. Between her wide-set green eyes and a sculpted mouth, his brother's male guests could be forgiven for halting mid-conversation to drink in the sight before them.

The female guests pretended without success not to notice the goddess floating about in Guy and Chantelle's house.

The scenario would be laughable if Raoul weren't one of the males affected by her femininity, which was even more provocative because she was modestly dressed in a summery outfit and seemed oblivious to the sensation she created. But he knew better. A woman who looked like her understood precisely the power she wielded.

Raoul had been targeted by such a woman in his early twenties and had come close to ruining his life because of her. Back then he'd become too physically enamored of her to read the signs, but fortunately he had discovered the truth behind her facade just in time. She'd lied about everything including her name, and had hoped to make Raoul husband number three and live the rest of her life in comfort.

Though it had come as a bitter blow to his pride, he'd survived and had finally gotten her out of his system. When he had met Danielle he had been immediately attracted, and since she came from a good family with money and didn't need his, he was able to let his guard down and had proposed to her shortly after.

Another fatal mistake. In time his supposedly adoring wife had turned out to be a much worse liar. It had spelled the end of their marriage, and no amount of pleading could ever resurrect the feelings he'd once had for her.

One of the maids offered him a glass of wine. Raoul turned her down, needing something a lot stronger. "How long will she be here?"

"She's been working on assignment in Europe. I have no idea how soon she has to get back to her job."

But not to her husband? Raoul mused cynically. She stood five foot seven, maybe eight, a height he discovered held an appeal he hadn't consciously thought about until now. Again he chided himself for noticing something that shouldn't even have played in his mind.

"What does she do?" Besides save lives…

Maurice took another sip from his wineglass. "I wouldn't know. The choking incident took precedence over everything. Guy asked us to keep Paul occupied while he accompanied her to her hotel."

Ciel! Terrific marriage the woman had. What was Guy thinking? Through shuttered eyes he tracked her movements. "Where's she from?"

"Southern California."

The mold of her body ruled out her being a supermodel. She was probably a grade-B actress who didn't have to act to get a part. All she needed to do was walk and breathe.

His jaded gaze flicked to his sister-in-law who sat composed in the wheelchair drinking her wine, looking young and elegant. And untouchable…

When Raoul thought about the drastic change in her since the accident, his gut twisted. She didn't need any more trauma. What in the name of all that was holy was Guy doing bringing this woman into their home? The sooner Mrs. Aldridge boarded her flight and left, the better.

He was about to ask more details, but Guy had spotted him standing next to Maurice and escorted his esteemed guest toward him, cupping her elbow with a familiarity Raoul found disturbing, if not repellant.

"Raoul? I'd like you to meet Laura Aldridge. Laura? This is my younger brother, Raoul, the brains of the family. She's the woman who saved my life yesterday."

"So I heard," he murmured, striving to keep his voice steady when what he really wanted to do was take his brother aside and demand an honest explanation. He reached for Mrs. Aldridge's hand, noticing she didn't wear a wedding ring. *"Enchanté, Madame,"* he said on purpose.

Only a woman who was confident in herself would give him a substantial shake in return, yet her hand with its tapered fingers and manicured nails was soft and well shaped…like the rest of her. When Raoul realized where his thoughts had wandered, he cursed inwardly.

"How do you do, Mr. Laroche," she responded

in a polite but dismissive voice, as if she knew he'd been assessing her and didn't like it.

That, plus the surprising intelligence coming from her eyes and expression put his teeth on edge. "It's fortunate for the Laroche family that you save lives in your spare time."

She smiled easily, but it was meant for Guy's benefit. "It's one of the things I do for a living."

Intrigued in spite of his growing frustration over his reaction to her he said, "You're an EMT then?"

Guy grew serious. "Laura is a part-time lifeguard at Manhattan Beach in California."

Like *Baywatch,* Raoul mused. He recalled the reruns from the famous American television show of the late eighties. He imagined most Frenchmen had derived pleasure from watching the female lifeguards plunge into the Southern Californian surf and come back out again. "I didn't realize the Heimlich maneuver was used in those kinds of saves."

Her body language didn't change, but her dark-fringed eyes turned a deeper green. "It isn't."

"Which makes me even more blessed," Guy murmured, his gaze focused on her in a kind of adoration Raoul hoped Chantelle couldn't see from where she was sitting. It seemed a great deal had gone on in his brother's world while Raoul had been away on business the last few days.

"It truly was miraculous," Maurice chimed in.

Guy nodded. "I want you to be the first to know that Laura has made arrangements to take some time off work, so she's going to be our house guest for a couple of weeks while Françoise is on vacation. I'm hoping her presence will be good for Chantelle."

Raoul needed a moment to recover from the stunning news. Something didn't add up here. Last evening was the first time Guy had met this woman. Raoul didn't buy it. What self-respecting stranger would accept an invitation like the one Guy had offered within a day of meeting each other?

Perhaps Mrs. Aldridge and Guy's relationship had begun before Chantelle's accident, and maybe Chantelle understood much more than anyone guessed. This would certainly explain the drastic change in her behavior. If so, his brother was playing a very dangerous game that was so unlike him, Raoul felt as if he'd just been kicked through a stone rampart.

His thoughts reeled. More than ever he was suspicious of the whole situation his brother had orchestrated with Mrs. Aldridge's blatant eagerness. While her lips curved in a faint smile at Guy's announcement, a tight band constricted Raoul's chest, but he couldn't afford to let his brother see he was affected by the unsettling events.

Was it possible his brother had been hiding an affair that had been going on for some time? Had she arranged to sit near him yesterday while he faked the choking incident, thus giving him an excuse to bring her into the home he'd made with Chantelle? It was as if they'd had a longtime association and only now had decided to make it public.

For years Raoul had considered that Chantelle

and his brother had the perfect marriage, which included a wonderful son. He'd never known two happier people. His own travesty of a union brought on by his wife's lies only highlighted the difference between them, or so he'd thought. *Mon Dieu*—had Raoul been wrong and his brother had only been putting on an act for everyone?

"How nice you have the kind of job that allows you that kind of freedom."

The classic line of her jaw became more delineated, as if his comment had reached its intended target and had disturbed her. "I'm very lucky to have such an understanding boss."

Not luck. There wasn't a man alive she couldn't enamor to the point he'd give her whatever she wanted—even Guy, the man Raoul had always looked up to for many reasons, especially for his high principles.

Raoul needed that stiff drink now. Focusing his gaze on his brother he said, "If you'll excuse me, I'll say hello to Chantelle." Maybe the mention of his wife's name might shame Guy back into paying attention to the woman he'd married, but his brother had Mrs. Aldridge on his mind and Raoul's comment passed him by.

After a brief look at the woman who'd managed to get beneath his skin the way no woman had ever done before, Raoul headed for the bar in the study off the living room. Hopefully a scotch would dull his senses, which had come alive the second he'd laid eyes on her. With fortification he might just be able to face his sister-in-law and not give himself away before he knew all the facts. Raoul intended to have Mrs. Aldridge investigated, because blind or sighted, a man could be excused for succumbing to her, but what did Guy really know about her. With her particular talents, she'd already gotten him to move her into his house.

"Raoul?"

He tossed back his drink before turning to Maurice who'd followed him. *"Oui?"*

"Can we talk for a minute?"

"*Bien sur.* Let's go out by the pool." He opened

the doors that led to the patio area where they could be strictly alone. "What's on your mind?"

"Your brother."

He was working up to something. It was possible that like Raoul, Maurice had come to the realization Guy had done something stupid and was going through a midlife crisis. Guy and Maurice had been friends for years. Maybe he could shed some light on his sudden, aberrant behavior.

Raoul eyed him for a moment. "I'm worried about him, too."

"He's so desperate at this point, I'm afraid he's grasping at straws."

Grasping at straws?

That wasn't exactly what he'd expected to hear from Maurice. Raoul rubbed the back of his neck in an effort to collect his thoughts.

Was Raoul the only one who could see what was going on here? If so it was because a woman had made a fool of him years ago and he'd learned his lesson.

There was no doubt the situation was desperate. A woman who looked like Mrs. Aldridge wasn't safe around any woman's husband. Another vision of her swam before his eyes.

"Yvette thinks there's too much of an age difference for this to work," Maurice explained. "I tend to agree with her."

Ah. Now he understood. Maurice had seen the writing on the wall. The clever man had used his wife and Chantelle's friend, Yvette, for the excuse to warn Raoul about this woman Guy had installed in the house. A younger woman who'd never be able to relate to Chantelle? But of course that wasn't what he'd really meant. Maurice was too discreet for that.

Suddenly Raoul felt a distaste for this conversation that bordered on gossip. "In the end it's Guy's call isn't it," he muttered, wanting to be loyal to the brother he loved. "Now I'm afraid you'll have to excuse me. After my trip, I need sleep."

He took off for his own villa one swift stride at a time.

CHAPTER TWO

ONCE Guy's brother had left the villa, Laura could breathe more easily and circulated among the guests. The second she'd sensed his piercing black gaze focused on her, she'd felt tension. No…it was more than that. He clearly didn't like her and she didn't know why.

It shouldn't have mattered one way or the other, yet across the crowded room she'd been perplexed by the hostility she'd felt coming from the brooding, olive-skinned male who stood an easy three inches taller than Guy. Certain body-type characteristics linked them as family, but not so their coloring. Instead of brown hair like Guy's, Raoul's longish, almost unruly black hair with dark whorls against his neck, framed brows of the exact color.

He wore the same expensive kind of clothes as his brother, but there the resemblance ended. It was her impression that beneath the silk material covering his chest breathed a physique containing a power barely leashed.

She wouldn't call him handsome. He was much more than that, but on an entirely different level. Gallic to his aquiline facial features, he exuded an overwhelming male sensuality her body responded to in spite of her efforts to remain unaffected.

Thankful she was no longer the object of his intense male scrutiny, she finished talking to one of the guests and walked over to Chantelle, who was surrounded by several of her female friends including Yvette from the Palio. They chatted, trying to draw her in, but Chantelle remained completely uninvolved, almost as if the party was not happening.

Laura sat down in a nearby chair and massaged her temples where she could feel a headache coming on. To her surprise Chantelle said, “I have painkiller if you need some, Laura. Come with me.”

Laura hadn’t realized Chantelle had been watching her, and her offer was an unexpected glimpse of the woman she had once been. Whatever had prompted it, Laura jumped at the chance to get on the old footing with Chantelle if it was possible.

“I could use some relief. Thank you.”

She followed Chantelle, whose surprised friends parted so she could move her wheelchair out of the salon. Guy caught Laura’s glance and nodded as if to say he was pleased with this much progress.

Chantelle had mastered the art of maneuvering her wheelchair over the Turkish rug covering the marble floor. She fairly whizzed out of the salon and down the right wing of the villa to the apartment where she and Guy lived. Before Laura could open the doors, Chantelle had already done it herself and rolled through the lavishly appointed sitting room to a table where she kept a bottle of pills.

"Take this." She handed it to Laura. "I have more in my bedroom if you need them."

"Thanks so much."

"You're welcome." She flashed Laura a glance. "I saw Raoul talking to you earlier. He's been very protective of me since the accident and can be quite forbidding sometimes, but don't let him scare you off, Laura. Raoul has his own demons he needs to deal with. Guy brought you to our home at my request. Raoul has his own home. Your being here is none of his business. Good night. I hope you sleep well."

Laura had been warned and dismissed. "I'm sure I shall. I hope you do too. Good night."

All the way to her own suite, Laura rehearsed everything Chantelle had told her about Guy's brother. She hadn't worked out whether Chantelle liked Raoul or not, but several things had become perfectly clear.

Not only were Chantelle's mental faculties razor sharp, but this was a house full of secrets. Laura had the premonition that in accepting their invitation, she'd walked into the middle of a war zone where there were landmines ready to go off with one misstep. The trick was to survive for the next two weeks without getting blown up in the process.

She took two pills, intending to go to bed, but she was too worked up to go to sleep yet. A swim in the pool sounded the perfect antidote for insomnia.

After removing her clothes, she slipped on the one-piece white suit she always wore as a lifeguard. With a towel over one arm she walked down the stairs off the veranda to the patio. She put her towel on a lounger before jumping into the water. The tepid temperature delighted her, and with a sigh she lay back and kicked her feet. In this position she could look up at the blue canopy above with its thumbnail moon and twinkling stars. Sheer paradise.

When she reached the edge, she turned on her stomach to do laps, needing the exercise. Back and forth she went at full speed, feeling the tension leave her body, but near the other side she collided with a hard-muscled male body and felt strong arms go around her, pulling her against him.

A soft gasp escaped her throat. She lifted her head to discover Raoul's dark face just centimeters from hers.

"I…I didn't realize you were in the pool," she stammered like an idiot.

"My villa is on the other side of the hedge. I dived in before noticing you," came his deep, grating voice.

The brothers lived out of each other's pockets. More than ever she understood Chantelle's warning.

His black hair was sleeked away from his forehead, revealing the masculine beauty of his bone structure. The combination of scents from the soap he'd used earlier and the fragrance of her shampoo wafted in the air surrounding them.

Without being able to touch bottom, their bodies brushed against each other. As his powerful legs tangled with hers, she felt an unexpected quickening of desire so intense, she could hardly breathe. The flicker in his black eyes meant he'd registered her reaction. This close to him she couldn't hide the charge of electricity arcing through her. It didn't help that the dusting of black hair on his chest and legs reminded her just how male he was.

Her attraction to him was so potent, it was humiliating. She flung herself out of his arms and kept swimming until she reached the other end of the pool. When she raised her head, she discovered Raoul waiting for her, not in the least winded. He examined her through slumberous eyes. "Shall we race ten laps? The winner can choose the prize."

Laura was intelligent enough not to get into any kind of race with him because he'd win, and she wasn't up to handling the kind of prize she was sure he had in mind. "It has been a long day. I'm afraid I'm too tired to be at my best. Perhaps you should ask Paul. He sings your praises."

Not willing to prolong this conversation, she executed a backward somersault and swam to the other end of the pool. After climbing out to get her towel she didn't look back, but she still felt a pair of penetrating black eyes follow her progress back to her room.

A quick shower and shampoo did nothing to relieve her heightened senses. In his arms she'd come alive. It was shocking to realize she could respond like that when she thought those feelings were permanently dead. On his part he'd done nothing to make her aware of him. He didn't have to. Raoul Laroche was one of those men endowed with traits irresistible to women.

After washing out her suit, she got ready for bed. But when she climbed under the covers, she lay awake for a long time troubled by the sensations still passing through her body. Pure physical chemistry had a lot to answer for. It had little to do with liking or disliking him.

Her mind insisted on going over the interrogation Raoul had put her through earlier in the evening. Every comment or question had stretched the boundaries of civility, and Laura couldn't help but wonder if he was this unpleasant to every stranger he met or if she was the exception.

The two brothers were the pillars of the Laroche financial world. Maybe they were too closely connected and the lines between their professional and personal lives became blurred more often than was healthy.

Judging by Chantelle's remarks, Raoul had a history of issues. Though it might explain his acerbic disposition to a point, Laura was at a loss to understand the caustic edge that had been directed at her personally. She wasn't mistaken about that.

She wasn't mistaken about the fire he'd lit, either. He'd held on to her a little too long for someone who couldn't stand her. Of course, men had an easier time separating their rational thoughts from their physical drives, but Laura wished she could view that moment in the pool with the same sangfroid as Raoul.

He wouldn't have trouble going to sleep tonight. There'd been a number of beautiful women at Guy's party who could make any man's pulse race including his, but it wouldn't mean anything more to him than the pleasure of the fleeting moment.

She hadn't seen a wedding ring on his finger, which meant Raoul was either a bachelor or divorced. Maybe even separated and waiting for his freedom like Laura. Depending on who asked for the divorce, he could be impatient to be let out of his prison, or dying inside because he was still in love with the woman he'd married.

If he was like Guy, it was probably the latter. That might account for his jaded, pointed remarks meant to inflict pain because he was hurting.

Troubled by Guy's dark, aloof brother, who unfortunately lived on the estate and shared the pool, Laura turned on her side, willing sleep to come. From now on she'd swim during the day to avoid another encounter like tonight. That way there'd be no accidental coming together in the pool, catching her totally off guard.

For one insane moment she'd thought he had been going to kiss her. What was more insane was that she wouldn't have stopped him. How bad was that? The temptation to taste his mouth had left her breathless.

Those feelings happened between near strangers all the time. It was called lust, a word she'd heard all her life, but had never experienced until tonight. Such feelings were wrong. Even though he'd been borderline cruel to her, somewhere deep inside she knew he would make a gratifying lover.

Ashamed of her thoughts, she turned on her stomach and pulled the pillow over the back of her head in the hope of warding them off.

Since the moment Laura had left the pool, Raoul had done twenty laps in order to exhaust himself before going to bed. He'd purposely run into her in order to provoke a response, yet it was Raoul who'd been the one affected.

His ploy to keep her in the pool longer had failed. Worse, the fact that Paul's name came so easily to her lips rankled. If this workout didn't help him sleep, then he'd have to resort to something medicinal.

As he heaved himself out of the water, he heard his brother say, "Raoul? What are you doing here?"

You mean what am I doing out here when I have my own pool?

That was a good question.

Of course, Raoul could have asked a few salient questions of Guy. What made the situation so precarious was the fact that there was only one reason his brother had sauntered out here in his swim trunks.

Like hungry sharks, two grown men were lurking in waters while they circled around a certain woman's bedroom. Viewed from a distance, the scene was appalling. Laura had made fools of them both.

"Paul asked me to swim with him earlier." It was only the truth. "But when I came out here to find him, he was gone. How did Chantelle handle the party?"

Guy walked over to him, his towel slung over one shoulder. "I don't know. She was asleep when I looked in on her. Did Laura swim with you?"

Was that jealousy Raoul detected?

Guy would be shocked if he knew what Raoul hadn't done with her but wanted to. *Ciel!*

The idea that his brother could be having an intimate relationship with her made Raoul see black. "She did a few laps and went in the house."

"So she didn't say anything about Chantelle?" Guy sounded worried. He should be. In fact he ought to be petrified!

"Why would she?"

Guy ran a hand through his hair. "During the party they left the salon together. I was wondering what they talked about."

Raoul shrugged. "I guess you'll have to ask her in the morning," he said pointedly. "That *is* the reason you invited her here, to be a companion to Chantelle, *n'est-ce pas?*"

His brother nodded.

About now a confession was called for. A little sign of remorse for what he was doing to his wife, not even behind her *back* at this point! But no such words passed his lips. Instead, much to Raoul's chagrin, the disappointed look on his face betrayed his true agenda.

Guy had no shame, yet with Raoul watching, his brother couldn't very well walk up the veranda steps to Laura's bedroom. For Chantelle's sake the knowledge that Guy couldn't be with Laura tonight filled Raoul with relief. On a purely personal note it pleased him no end.

"It looks like you won't be needing this." Raoul reached for his brother's towel. Taking his time, he began to dry himself off. No way did he intend to leave the patio until Guy had gone. Tonight's assignation had been foiled. Raoul had zero sympathy for his brother.

"I may be late going into the office in the morning," Guy muttered, showing strains of being beaten. There was no 'may' about it. With Laura living on the premises, it was doubtful the company would see him for the next two weeks.

"I'm afraid I won't be there either. Jean-Luc wants me to look over that complex in Antibes. Why don't you go with me? We'll decide if we want to buy it. With Laura keeping Chantelle company, you can get away for a little while without worrying."

Maybe on the drive he could get his brother to break down and tell him what was going on. They'd never kept secrets from each other in their lives.

Guy shook his head. "Not this time. You go ahead." In the next breath he left the patio, his mind and thoughts elsewhere.

Raoul stayed where he was. Part of him was torn up inside to see the change in Guy. The other part felt disgust over his possible romantic involvement with the woman Raoul couldn't get out of his mind. Laura Aldridge was almost fifteen years younger than Guy. On the loose in Europe, he wondered how many other men she'd ensnared before targeting his brother.

As Raoul had learned, a woman like that didn't have to earn a living. He doubted Laura even had a real job. That business about getting her boss's permission was a con if he'd ever heard one. She lived off her victims. When she'd had enough and was bored, she moved on to the next poor devil whose bank account held a twelve-figure balance. Why couldn't Guy see this?

Tomorrow he'd phone his attorney. It wouldn't hurt to run a check on the American woman. She might not be who she said she was. She might even have a police record on both sides of the Atlantic.

After their parents had died years ago, Guy had always looked after Raoul. Now it was Raoul's turn to protect his brother from a possible predator who had the kind of face and body to tempt every strata of saint down to sinner.

The next morning one of the maids led Laura to a patio off the dining room, where Chantelle was seated. It overlooked a fabulous, multicolored rose garden. She'd smelled their fragrance last evening and couldn't get enough of it.

"*Bonjour,* Laura."

"*Bonjour,* Chantelle." she said back, trying to imitate the sounds. More than ever she marveled at this family. They all spoke English so well. She couldn't imagine learning French with the same fluency.

Her hostess had already wheeled herself to the rectangular glass table supported by ornate wrought iron legs. Laura put her sketchpad down against one of them and took a seat across from her while another maid served them breakfast. The patio having a western exposure, they were shaded from the hot sun.

"How did you sleep?"

"Once the pills worked, I passed out. Thank you for giving them to me. I need to go to a pharmacy and get some of my own."

"Anything you need, all you have to do is ask."

"That's very kind of you."

Like Laura, Chantelle had dressed in a white knit top and matching shorts. She looked cool and perfectly beautiful. Laura's heart felt a wrench to realize that beneath her facade lived an emotionally frozen woman.

"These croissants melt in your mouth."

Chantelle flashed her an unexpected smile. "I'll tell the chef."

Laura chuckled. "To be honest, I feel like I'm in fantasyland."

"I've been there."

"I know. I tended little Paul while you and Raoul walked around Disneyland. You have no idea how much I envied you your wonderful husband and son. Yours was the kind of marriage I wanted one day."

When Chantelle didn't respond to her remarks Laura said, "Actually I'm talking about a completely different place. Your home is a fantasyland—out of this world. Those rose beds are so perfect. You must have the best gardeners on the Côte d'Azur."

"Before my accident, I did all the weeding myself. Now I have to tell them how to do their job. They miss too many."

"Let me do it while I'm here—" she blurted.

Chantelle cocked her dark head. "You like gardening?"

"I remember talking to you about the grandmother who raised me, but I probably didn't mention that we lived in a little forties bungalow in Manhattan Beach. She loved flowers and had me out working alongside her when I was just a girl. It was the one job I loved most, probably because it was outside."

"Is she still alive?"

"No. She died eight years ago. I kept up the yard until I got married. My husband convinced me to sell it. I haven't done any gardening since."

Laura wouldn't have listened to Ted except that a developer was planning to buy the whole strip of houses around there and build a mall. The price being offered was better than what an individual buyer might pay for it. That had been Ted's reasoning at the time.

After she had reluctantly sold it, the project had fallen through, but she had a feeling Ted had known it would. He just didn't want her holding on to her memories. Everything to do with him had been a mistake.

Not liking the direction of her thoughts, she munched on the chilled honeydew melon, her favorite.

Chantelle eyed her over the rim of her coffee. "If you're serious about the weeding, be my guest."

"I already am." They both smiled at the same time. "It would make me very happy to get out there so I can feel useful. My hands are itching to dig into the soil."

"I know the feeling."

How sad that Chantelle could admit to such a thing, yet she refused to act on it.

"Tomorrow I'll ask the gardener to bring you some gloves and thc things you'll need."

"Thank you."

"I believe there's an artist in anyone who loves gardening. After you've finished eating, may I see what you've been sketching?"

Guy had hoped Laura would draw his wife out, but so far Chantelle was the one forcing Laura to open up.

"I'll show you now." She reached for the pad and handed it to her.

After Chantelle flipped the cover over, a soft gasp escaped her lips. She studied the top page, then began thumbing through the others. Finally she raised her head. Her eyes were shining. For just a moment, she was like the old Chantelle.

"You've captured the whole Palio—the people…the costumes…the horses…the city—You're a genius!"

"No—"

"Indeed you are. What medium do you work with when you make these life-size? Oil? Watercolor?"

"Neither. I studied graphic design in college. After I graduated, I went to work for a video game company in California. My job is to provide interesting backgrounds for games which other people in the company develop."

"Video games? Like the ones my son plays, much to my disgust?"

"I'm afraid so," Laura admitted. "The technology is so advanced, the industry has taken off. With my pencil I create backgrounds for all ages. This one on the Palio will be used as a horse race obviously. Each horse and rider runs through a separate part of the town with many obstacles to overcome. My job is to find unusual places that suggest games to me."

"Where else have you been?" Chantelle actually sounded interested and Laura could glimpse shades of her former self.

"Two months ago I spent a week in Hamlin, Germany, to create a background for a children's game. It's an adorable town with a lot of carvings. My grandmother read me all the fairy tales. One of my favorites was 'The Pied Piper.' I came up with the idea of him leading all the children out of the town and the player has to prevent them from following him by using various methods that take a certain amount of skill.

"After leaving there I went to Holland for a week to sketch the windmills and old gabled houses for another game about stopping the holes in the dikes."

Chantelle shook her head. "But this is remarkable! *You* are remarkable!"

"No, but I must admit it's a lot of fun to get paid a commission for doing something I love. In between times, I still work part-time as a lifeguard at the beach. As you can imagine, I've done the sketches for an underwater video game for children. It involves a merman." An image of Raoul in the pool suddenly flashed into her mind, causing her to take an extra breath.

"When do you have time to see your husband?"

At the mention of Ted, Laura shuddered. "My two-year marriage failed almost from the start, Chantelle. He's an attorney from a political family, but he assured me he wasn't interested in politics. I told him I didn't want to be married to a politician and put him off for a long time until I was convinced he meant it.

"A few months into our marriage I learned he'd always planned to run for Congress. Everything had been a lie. He didn't love me, all he wanted was to parade me in front of people, something I abhor.

"Six months ago, after I learned he'd been with other women, I found the strength to leave him and file for divorce. He's refusing to give me one, but in time I'll get it and he won't have a choice."

"Bravo!" Chantelle exclaimed. "Once a liar, always a liar." She said it with such vehemence, Laura had the idea Chantelle was speaking from personal experience. But surely it wasn't anything to do with Guy….

"In Ted's case it's true." Her gaze flicked to her hostess. "He's nothing like your husband, who absolutely adores you."

The second the words left her lips, the atmosphere changed. Chantelle handed her back the sketchpad.

Laura couldn't bear the thought that Guy might have lied about something that could have hurt his wife so profoundly. In fact she refused to believe it. "Has he left for his office, or will he be joining you?"

"He's in his study on a conference call."

"Lucky you to have him at home." Whether it irked Chantelle or not, Laura had said it. "What are your plans today?"

"I'm having my massage in a half hour, then my hair done. Later I plan to do some reading out here."

"Mind if I sketch while you read? The rose garden, in fact your whole villa with that maze around the back, has given me an idea for a children's game, but only with your permission of course."

"What's it about?" Chantelle sounded pleased by the idea.

"It's not fully formed in my mind yet. Maybe later you can help me brainstorm."

"You wouldn't mind?"

"Mind what?"

The interjection of a silky male voice sent a small shiver through Laura. She didn't have to turn her head to know who'd come out on the patio.

"*Bonjour,* Raoul. What's going on around here? Doesn't anyone have to go to work anymore? After being in Switzerland, I would have thought you'd be in your office at the crack of dawn. Instead here you are and Guy's still on the phone in the den."

Laura watched him move around the table to kiss his sister-in-law's cheek. Dressed in a black silk shirt and gray trousers that molded his powerful legs, he looked incredible. “I’m on my way to Antibes on business and thought maybe you and Laura might like to go with me. You could do a little shopping. We’ll pack your wheelchair.”

“Not today. I have other plans, but I’m sure Laura would enjoy getting out.”

Laura’s heartbeat sped up at the mere idea of being alone with him. “That’s very thoughtful of you, Chantelle, but I’m perfectly happy here.” Guy was counting on her.

“Nonsense. You won’t be gone all day, will you, Raoul?”

“That depends.”

Laura had a feeling he’d said that just to get under her skin. Nothing had changed since last night. She could still feel his antipathy.

“Go with him, Laura. The drive might give you more ideas. Paul and his friends will be around. I’ll be busy keeping an eye on them.”

For some reason Chantelle wanted to be left alone and she didn’t care if she pushed Laura on to her complicated brother-in-law. Maybe Laura had offended her by saying what she had about Guy. It probably felt like she was pressuring her.

If any progress was going to be made with his wife, she needed to refrain from talking about her husband in front of her. No matter how anxious Guy was to bring his wife around to her normal self, Laura's grandmother would remind her of the old adage about eating an elephant one bite at a time.

"By your silence, one would assume you're afraid to go with me," Raoul mocked before devouring a croissant. "I promise not to drive off into the sunset with you, Mrs. Aldridge. Whatever would Mr. Aldridge say."

"*Assez,* Raoul! If you keep this up, she'll get the wrong impression."

"What impression?" His hooded gaze swerved to Laura. "Is that true?" After asking the question, he proceeded to eat a small bunch of purple grapes.

For some perverse reason he enjoyed needling

her. Unfortunately, Chantelle wasn't being any help. Laura had the distinct feeling she enjoyed the repartee. The two of them shared a unique relationship she couldn't begin to understand.

Making a decision not to be a part of it, she stood up from the chair and reached for her sketchpad. "How soon did you want to leave?"

From the gleam in his dark eyes, her question had pleased him. "Right now."

"Then give me a minute to change."

His gaze traveled over her in lazy appraisal. "You look fine as you are."

"Thank you, but if I'm going to do any shopping, I'd feel more comfortable in a skirt. Where shall I meet you?"

"I'll bring my car around the front of the villa."

"Give me five minutes." She looked at Chantelle. "While I'm out, is there something I can pick up for you? A book you've been wanting to read?"

"Nothing for me."

"A special treat then?"

Chantelle flashed her a smile. "That's very sweet. Thank you for offering, but *non merci.*"

Laura planned to bring her back something anyway. Her gaze flicked to Raoul who was eyeing her strangely. "I won't be long."

His lips twisted. "Did you hear that, Chantelle?"

She chided him without rancor, "Not all women are as impossible as you choose to believe. A woman as lovely as Laura doesn't need to primp."

Not wanting to hear any more, Laura left the patio to change into her wraparound skirt in a taupe color with white trim. Before coming to breakfast she'd caught her hair back in a ponytail with a white scarf. Because she thought she'd be in the house with Chantelle all day, she hadn't bothered with makeup.

She wouldn't bother now. Raoul Laroche would have to take her as she was. Hopefully her demeanor didn't reveal her highly emotional state. It wouldn't do for Raoul to know how much his nearness affected her.

After filling her tote bag with supplies, she made her way to the front of the house before the five minutes were up. No sooner had she closed the door behind her than she saw a white cabriolet Porsche wheel around the drive.

A cry of alarm escaped her lips. How had Ted found her? How did he get past the security guard? For a moment she felt sick to her stomach.

CHAPTER THREE

RAOUL was surprised to discover Laura waiting for him. To find a woman ready on time had to be a first. He coasted to a stop.

However, the sight of her champagne hair and unmistakable figure made him slow to realize she had a pallor that hadn't been there when she'd left the table. He had a suspicion she'd seen Guy on her way out and they'd had words. To learn Laura was leaving the villa with Chantelle's blessing in order to go with Raoul must have upset his brother.

Pleased to have foiled another attempt for Guy to be alone with her, Raoul reached across the seat to open the passenger door for her. She looked good. Most women past their teens couldn't get away without wearing makeup, but she carried it off perfectly.

Beneath the attractive skirt, her gorgeous long legs were bare. Much to his chagrin he could find nothing artificial about her. The more she underplayed her looks, the more she stood out like a fresh peach warming in the sun, all pink and golden.

Her arm brushed against his as she fastened her seat belt. His body quickened at the contact. The recurring sensation wasn't supposed to happen. Once she closed the door, he put the car in gear and took off without saying anything. He followed the winding drive flanked by cypress trees until they passed the guardhouse and came out on the coast road.

After a few minutes he said, "If Chantelle had come with us, I would have brought the sedan. Do you mind the top down? I can always put it up."

"That's up to you. Frankly I like being able to see all around," she responded without looking at him.

The women he knew didn't want to be blown about, but as he was finding out with Laura, she wasn't your typical female. She didn't talk incessantly, a quality that should have pleased him since they were going to be together for as long as he felt like keeping her away from Guy. Yet the fact that she appeared so relaxed with him actually irritated him.

"This area isn't that much different from your coast in Southern California."

"It's completely different," she countered. "The ocean and the sea can't be compared." Having been to California on several occasions, he privately agreed with her. "All those ancient little villages I saw from the helicopter tucked away high in the Maritime Alps create a charm like no place else on earth."

He hadn't realized Guy had flown her here in the helicopter. That was an unprecedented move on his part. His brother was in deep.

She recrossed her legs, probably on purpose. Among other things it drew his attention to the bone-colored leather sandals encasing her feet. No toenail polish. Everything *au naturel.* So far he couldn't see anything he didn't like and he'd been trying!

"You've traveled in Europe before?"

"Some, but not along the Riviera. It's breathtaking."

Raoul hated to admit *she* was too. The truth of it shook him almost as much as the fact that she didn't give anything away she didn't want him to know.

He came to the turn for Cros de Cagnes and veered left to follow the coast road. "What is it you do for a living…besides rescue drowning victims?"

She put on a pair of sunglasses. "I draw landscapes to create backgrounds for video games."

Video games? Raoul had to admit that was one answer he would never have expected. "What genre?" She was an artiste all right, but the kind she was alluding to came as a revelation, if it were true.

"Mostly for children and young adults."

"No war games?"

"If you mean the kind guys from eighteen to thirty play all day and all night long, then no."

Whether she was conning him or not, he couldn't help but chuckle because what she'd said was so true. After she gave him some examples, he was prompted to ask the name of the company she worked for.

"Other World Video Games. You've probably never heard of it."

"I can't say I have." So far she'd picked something so safe, he couldn't accuse her of lying until he'd researched it. "How long have you been doing that kind of work?"

"Since college."

"Did you get a degree?"

She nodded. "Graphic design."

While his mind did the math he remembered something. "At breakfast I saw you with a sketchpad."

"Yes. It's filled with drawings of Siena and the

Palio. I was working on a scene when your brother started to choke. Chantelle wanted to see it."

To his dismay, every time he asked her a question, she answered it without hesitation. If she had things to hide, he wouldn't know it from her seemingly forthright manner. So far she hadn't asked anything of him. The idea that she was merely tolerating him didn't sit well.

Raoul kept telling himself he was doing this for Guy's sake, but a part of him knew that wasn't totally true. Laura Aldridge had captured his attention in too many ways to lie to himself.

Earlier this morning he'd phoned his attorney and asked him to run a background check on her. Louis promised to get back to him when he had any solid information. In the meantime it was up to Raoul to learn what he could from the woman herself. If he asked more personal questions, maybe he could get her to squirm. That's what he was looking for, to catch her in something that would give away her agenda.

"How do you balance your work and marriage?"

After a quiet interval, she said, "I don't."

That's right. She only had time to concentrate on ruining someone else's. Her refusal to play his game had just raised the stakes. He took the next right that brought them into Juan-les-Pins, an extension of Antibes.

"I'm going to check out a complex of buildings in the yachting district that our company might purchase for our export line. It won't take me long. Afterward I'll drive us through Vence to one of those little villages you referred to. We'll have a late lunch and do whatever we feel like."

She nodded as if amenable, but he felt her tension because she'd only been putting up with him until they returned to the villa. He could tell by the rigidity of her body that her patience was wearing thin. That was the crack in the veneer he'd been waiting for.

"Would you like me to stop and get you a drink first?"

"No, thank you. I have a bottle of water in my bag if I get thirsty."

Still no eye contact. To travel around Europe alone picking up vulnerable men, she'd learned to be independent. It was part of her mystique, another intriguing trait he hated to acknowledge.

A few minutes later he pulled up to the entry of an empty warehouse and parked the car alongside a bank of palm trees. They'd shield her from the sun while he was inside. Jean-Luc, their company's real estate agent, was already in front of the doors waiting for him.

As soon as he saw them, the older man headed for the Porsche. One look at Laura and he started salivating. It put Raoul in mind of Guy, who would have had the same reaction when he'd seen Laura for the first time. The identical thing had happened to Raoul, causing his own desire and anger to flare.

On impulse and something else he couldn't put a name to yet, he leaned across the seat and kissed her full on her unsuspecting mouth. It happened so naturally she didn't have time to resist.

That was the idea. Jean-Luc was bearing down

on them. A picture was worth a thousand words, so they said. He was the biggest gossip on the Côte d'Azur. He had to be to stay in business. By tomorrow word would have reached Guy's ears that his brother was involved with a blond bombshell, and Guy's hands would be tied.

If he confronted Raoul, Guy would be admitting his own guilt. Though he'd be furious with him at first, it would expose Laura for the opportunist she was. One day Guy would thank him.

But Raoul's thoughts faded as the taste of her was all he'd imagined and more, prompting him to take his time until she tore her lips from his. "How dare you," she cried in a low tone.

Her outrage sounded genuine enough, but it came an instant too late because she'd started to respond to him before catching herself. It wasn't something you could hide. If she was supposed to be involved with Guy, what did her reaction to Raoul mean?

To his dismay another part of him didn't want to know the answer because for an insane moment he was enjoying himself too much. Raoul couldn't abide the thought of her responding to him and his brother, too. Yet that was why he'd done this experiment, to find out what kind of woman she really was.

He smiled. "Come on, Laura. After what almost happened in the swimming pool last night, we both know you didn't mind it all that much." Satisfied to see the rush of hot color sweep into her cheeks, he left her to her own devices while he levered himself from the car to intercept Jean-Luc.

Denied an introduction, his curious friend would be even more eager to know the identity of the new mystery woman in Raoul's life.

"Oh-la-la—" Jean-Luc clapped him on the shoulder as they walked toward the doors. "When your ex finds out about that one, she'll want to scratch her eyes out."

Raoul grinned despite his torment. "She can try…"

The other man's laughter rang in the air.

What Jean-Luc didn't know was that Danielle was no match for the woman whose lips were as soft and lush as the rest of her. In trying to protect Chantelle, it was guaranteed Raoul had opened himself up to an infinite number of sleepless nights and cold showers.

Laura couldn't stop the trembling. Though secretly thrilled to realize the desire she'd felt last night wasn't all on her side, she was also terrified. What if one of Ted's undercover agents had discovered where she was staying and had followed the Porsche to Antibes.

With a telephoto lens they could've taken pictures of Raoul kissing her. That kind of evidence could influence a judge into siding with Ted's attorney to hold up the case. Who knew how long it would take before she obtained her divorce? Laura didn't dare entertain a relationship with Raoul that could jeopardize everything she'd been working so hard for.

She reached in her bag and drained her bottle

of water in an effort to rid herself of the imprint of Raoul's hard mouth. Those male lips that could twist with mocking cruelty had covered hers with enough coaxing pressure to draw a spontaneous response she'd had no power to stop. Knowing that he had a distinct dislike for her made her physical reaction to him even more unacceptable.

Though their kiss had been real enough, she sensed he'd done it for the other man's benefit. To what end she didn't know. If Raoul was trying to frighten her off, he didn't have to wait until they had an audience. Things were more of a mystery than ever unless Chantelle was somehow behind all this.

It pained Laura to think that Chantelle might have asked her brother-in-law to find a way to get Laura to leave the villa without involving Guy. If she truly didn't want her husband's attentions, then of course she'd resent his bringing Laura into their home to try to help. Thinking back to this morning, Chantelle had been adamant that Laura go on the drive without her.

Laura could leave France tonight of course and probably ought to, but she owed Guy a truthful explanation. No matter what, her loyalty was to him. Yet to tell him what had happened today could also hurt him deeply if he didn't know his brother was working against him to get rid of Laura.

She couldn't figure it out. The two men's relationship had to be somewhat normal, didn't it? Otherwise Raoul wouldn't have been at the party. Surely if there was real animosity between them, the brothers wouldn't work together or live in such close proximity to each other.

Stymied by so many unanswered questions and the kiss that still haunted her, she came to the conclusion that all she could do was bluff her way through the next two weeks and avoid Raoul as much as possible. He liked making trouble, but she could give it back if she had to.

If things became impossible, she'd go to Guy and tell him she'd changed her mind about staying. To make a good case she'd tell him she didn't want his family involved in the event Ted found out where she was staying. Surely he'd understand that. Who knew what complications might arise that could upset Chantelle unnecessarily.

Laura was so deep in thought she didn't realize Raoul had returned until she heard the door open. In that brief moment she glanced around and their eyes met.

"You surprise me," he said after starting the car.

"What? That I didn't run away from you?" She sighed. "I've been kissed before by men I didn't know, even when I wasn't saving their lives." Enjoying turning this back on him she added, "If you were that anxious, you should have taken advantage while we were in the pool last night, but then I suppose you stopped short because you were afraid someone might be watching."

The car leaped ahead. His eyes burned like black fires. "Were you disappointed?"

"I think so."

"Only think?" he challenged.

For a moment he sounded playful rather than serious, catching her off guard. She couldn't help smiling.

If this was part of his game, he was good at it. He was gorgeous, too. The most beautiful man she'd ever met in her life. Southern California was full of them. Her husband, Ted, had stood out, but no one came close to the gut-wrenching sensuality of Raoul Laroche.

Then his eyes narrowed on her mouth before his expression hardened, causing lines to darken his features. He turned his attention back to the road leading out of the marina area and in a flash, when she'd felt buoyant for no reason, the moment disappeared as if it had never been.

Instead of the interrogation he'd subjected her to on the way to Antibes, he remained silent during the picturesque drive into the colorful hills with their patches of tuberose and jasmine. The tension between them was almost palpable, but until he explained himself, Laura had nothing to say.

Though she was tempted to ask him to take her home, her pride had gotten in the way. She didn't want him to think his tactics back there had succeeded in destroying her confidence.

The scent of flowers grew more intoxicating the higher they climbed to the craggy summits. His Porsche was made for these hairpin turns on narrow roads. He handled his car like a Formula 1 driver, removing the worry she wasn't safe. Any fear she harbored came from her own susceptibility to his potent charisma. Just watching the way the steering wheel responded beneath his strong hands, the fluid motion of his powerful body when he moved, brought her pleasure.

Before long they entered a quaint medieval village perched on a spur of land with a stream running through the rocky gorge below. The sign said Tourettes Sur Loup. She loved the unique names.

He pulled into a parking lot full of other cars

and turned off the motor. "I'm confident the artist in you will find something to purchase once we've eaten. The village is full of local artisan crafts."

She listened for that dreaded trace of mockery but didn't hear it. Relieved he'd decided not to hound her for the moment, she alighted from the car before he could help her. Laura would be all right if he didn't touch her. If someone was photographing them from a distance, she wouldn't provide them another opportunity to catch her in an intimate moment with Raoul.

They entered beneath an arched porte with a tall clock tower and followed the main street through the oldest part of the town filled with tourists. "The village was fortified in the Middle Ages," Raoul explained. "These are the only walls remaining."

"It's unreal," she cried softly, her gaze traveling down a sunken, stone-paved path centuries old.

He led them to a little café where they ate *steak aux frites* and topped it off with a *tarte à l'orange,* a village specialty. Replete after the delicious meal, they explored the myriad of shops displaying local crafts. Laura wanted to buy everything, but in the end she purchased nothing except an oval-shaped, locally woven basket full of violets that grew in the region. Their deep-purple color thrilled her.

"I'm paying for these," she announced, putting some Euros in the woman's hand before Raoul could pull the necessary bills from his wallet.

He eyed her skeptically. "You're sure this is all you want? You can't take flowers back to Los Angeles with you." Oh how politely he'd said the words, like he was speaking to a child. She got the impression he couldn't wait for her to announce her departure plans.

For a little while she'd forgotten that Raoul was her enemy, and with that reminder the enjoyment of the last hour vanished.

"They're for Chantelle." A thank-you gift for allowing her to stay in their home. "She misses puttering in her garden. I thought she might enjoy these." Laura buried her nose in the petals to inhale their sweet perfume.

When she lifted her head, she caught a look of something she couldn't decipher in those black depths before he took the basket from her. A small shiver ran through her as they retraced their steps to the car parked beyond the walled town.

After she climbed in, he placed the basket on the floor behind her seat where the flowers would be protected. This time she was careful not to look at him. That way she wouldn't be subjected to any more fiery darts of accusation.

Once again they were traveling along the back roads of Provence that were more alive and colorful than any painting she could ever create. They eventually passed through another charming town whose name she couldn't pronounce.

"This was the home of Marcel Pagnol," he informed her in a gravelly voice. "In case you don't know wh—"

"I know," she cut him off. "Hollywood made

his novels world famous. I've been seeing *Jean de la Florette* around every farmhouse and fountain."

By the shifting of gears she realized she'd irritated him. "You could have played the part of Manon. She was a child of nature, too."

"You mean the girl who had every man in the village lusting after her?" she inquired. She shook her head despairingly. "You might have spared me that."

Through the grimace he said, "You're the one who chose to read something negative into my remark. In my own apparently obtuse way I was attempting to pay you a compliment."

"You mean to make up for your uninvited advance in front of the real estate agent?"

His lips thinned in response. "I preferred Jean-Luc to think I was having an affair with you."

"Nice," she bit out. "There's nothing a woman loves more than to be considered a man's girl-toy. Yet I have to admit I'm surprised that a Frenchman like you who knows he's attractive and can obviously have his pick on a whim has to prove anything."

She smiled in satisfaction to see the way his fingers tightened on the wheel. Unable to resist she said, "Evidently your agent is a member of the good-old-boy's network. Every society in the world has them, especially among the exceptionally rich and famous.

"Are you hoping word of me will get back to your latest girlfriend? Or your wife? Or possibly your ex? Or maybe your almost ex? Now I have to ask myself if you're praying she'll finally leave you alone, or maybe this woman is another man's wife and you're counting on her jealousy to bring her to heel."

She heard a volley of French invective that needed no translation. "That's quite a tongue you've acquired."

"It's been sharpened on wealthy men like you who collect women like some people collect shells." The Stillman men led the pack.

"How many have there been?" he ground out.

"Thousands! However, I dare say that's not as many as your fertile imagination suspects." Laura laughed in pain. "Me thinks I'd better get myself away to a nunnery quick before you become my next victim. Heaven forbid, eh?"

"Heaven forbid," he muttered so morosely, she felt it to her bones. Ridiculous as it was, his repudiation stung.

They'd reached Nice and were following the signs for Cap Ferrat.

"Now that we've gotten all that out of the way, Raoul, maybe we can both enjoy the rest of the short drive back to the villa. The next time you decide to invite me anywhere, better not obey the urge or I'll know you're only lusting after me. For your information, that's the biggest turn-off to a woman there is."

He turned his head in her direction. "Then how do you explain your response when I kissed you?" came the slithering taunt.

The man was a devil. "Chemical reaction." Knowing what question he would ask next, she answered it. "And yes, it happens every time. It's my nature. You already called it and you'd be right because clearly you're a very intelligent man, so consider yourself warned."

She was sure he drove them above the speed limit to reach the villa. The second he pulled to a screeching halt, she got out of the car and reached for the basket of flowers. As she turned around Guy came down the steps to greet her. He waved to his brother.

The sight of him was like a balm to her soul and she flew toward him. He put his arm around her, flowers and all and smiled warmly at her. "How was your day?"

"I discovered it's true. Provence *is* God's garden. These are for Chantelle."

As he took the basket from her, his eyes misted. "Let's take them in to her. She'll love them."

Without a backward glance Laura walked into the foyer with him. The click of the door coincided with the squeal of tires out on the gravel.

Guy looked askance. “Did Raoul tear around with you the whole day like that?

Now would be the perfect time to confide in him about his brother, but she couldn’t do it. Whatever rush he got out of insulting her, it would grow old with time. She could outlast him.

“Of course not. I think he was anxious to get back to his villa for an important phone call with the agent.” Even if it was a lie, it was an innocent one. “Let me freshen up, then I’ll join you and Chantelle.”

“What did he think of the property?”

She averted her eyes. “I’m not sure. He didn’t really say. See you two in a few minutes.”

Once in the guest suite, Laura decided to phone her best friend in California, who lived in the apartment across the hall from her. Cindy, who’d been divorced for a year, was keeping an eye on her place and gathered the mail for her from the box downstairs. In case there was a bill she hadn’t taken care of, she needed to know about it and get it paid. Laura did the same thing for Cindy when she flew to Georgia to visit her family, and the two women had formed a close friendship. If Ted ever came to the apartment when Laura was out, Cindy documented the time so Laura could give the information to her attorney. There was a restraining order on him, but Ted chose to ignore it whenever he felt like it.

When she and Cindy played tennis or saw a film, they commiserated about the men in their lives and talked about the ideal man who would one day sweep them off their feet. One of these days Laura would confide in Cindy about Raoul, but she knew he was far from her ideal man. He was arrogant, frustrating and it was all right for him to make insinuations and ask all the impertinent questions he wanted, but she noticed he never did tell her one thing about himself. The very thought of him triggered a fresh spurt of adrenaline.

Restless as a caged animal, Raoul paced the rooms of his villa, but the bars were invisible.

He could step outside anytime he wanted—beyond the flowering hedge if he so desired—in order to have access to her.

He desired all right.

During their outing she'd been playing him with a master hand. The lines were so blurred at this point he didn't know what was truth and what was the lie. When she had rushed toward Guy like that, all the breath had left his lungs. His brother in turn had showed her the kind of tenderness he felt for someone he truly cared about, loved even.

Was that the result of her saving his life? Could the answer be as simple and as complicated as that?

In desperation he phoned Louis, but his attorney had left his office for the day. If he'd found the information Raoul had requested on her, he would have phoned him back by now anyway. It appeared he would have to wait a little longer.

An hour later, after a shower and shave, Raoul

decided to go over to Guy's and take him aside, lay it all out. He couldn't go on like this another twenty-four hours.

Laura had said she'd been in Europe before. If his brother had been having a long-term affair with her, then Raoul needed to convince him to give her up for all the obvious reasons. Chantelle would never get better if she thought she'd lost Guy.

His sister-in-law had guts and courage to welcome Laura into their home at her husband's request. But when she must surely be bleeding inside, how long could she keep up her convincing front?

More to the point, how long could Laura stay under that roof knowing her presence had to be crucifying Chantelle? He raked his hands through his hair, trying to fit all the pieces together, but that was the problem. Just when he thought one would go into place, he discovered it was the wrong piece or the wrong place.

Earlier when Laura had told him she was buying the violets for Chantelle, he could have sworn she'd done it out of kindness, nothing more. At one point the jabs and arrows had seemed to change to gentle teasing. Their conversation had slid in and out of context until he didn't know where he was with her.

Prepared for the fight Guy would put up, he left the house for his brother's. Raoul found the family eating dinner on the patio. The basket of violets served as the centerpiece. There was no sign of Laura.

"Hey, Uncle Raoul."

"Hey, yourself, Paul."

Chantelle looked up. "There you are. If you want to join us, I'll tell cook."

"I'm not hungry, *merci.*"

His brother, acting as if nothing was wrong, motioned for him to sit down. "How did it go with Jean-Luc? Was he right about the complex? You think it's worth purchasing?"

What a cool customer his brother was.

Raoul could only marvel. "I want a few days to think about it."

Guy nodded. "Thanks for taking Laura with you today. When I told her how much you dislike playing tour guide, she said she was doubly grateful for the way you put yourself out."

If that was a direct quote, and it sounded like it was, Raoul had reason to believe Laura had told Guy the truth, that his younger brother had trespassed on his private territory earlier today. That changed the timing of Raoul's agenda. He would wait and see what his brother did with the information when they were alone.

In case it brought Guy to his senses before things went any further, then it would have been worth it…even if Raoul would always be haunted by the memory of her mouth moving beneath his.

Chantelle swallowed the last of her tea. "Laura assured me she would treasure the memory of your trip to Tourettes. She's truly *une enfant de la nature* to bring me these violets."

At the reminder of their conversation about Manon, the hand in Raoul's pocket formed a fist. Incredibly it seemed Laura had won Chantelle's acceptance. Or had she? Was it all pretense?

He gazed around their little *tableau à trois*. While Paul ate his dinner oblivious to the tension, Guy sat there with no intention of giving anything away in front of Chantelle. She'd probably known about his extramarital affair for a long time. It was understandable why Laura hadn't yet made up the fourth to this *spectacle à Laroche*.

Getting to his feet he announced, "I'm going for a dip in the pool." Maybe Guy would follow him and demand an explanation. If not now, later.

At some point Laura had to make an appearance. Raoul had nothing to do but wait for everything to play out. He walked through the villa to the patio where he stripped down to his swim trunks and dived in. A good workout was what he needed to release his pent-up negative energy.

Ten minutes later he was finishing his laps

when Paul made an appearance from around the side of the house.

Raoul smiled at him from the other end. "*Salut, mon gars.*"

"Hi." His nephew, still dressed in shorts and a T-shirt, sat down on the edge and dangled his strong legs in the water.

"Did you have a good time at Claude's today?"

"It was okay. How long ago did she leave?"

Not sure he'd heard Paul correctly, Raoul swam across to him. "Did who leave? Your *maman* was sitting at the dinner table ten minutes ago."

"I meant Laura."

"I wasn't aware she'd gone anywhere." He hoped she was in her bedroom nursing a migraine over her guilt.

"She was going to start teaching me CPR, but I guess she forgot. The maid said Laura asked Pierre to drive her someplace in the limo so papa wouldn't have to leave *maman*."

That bit of news sent a shockwave through

Raoul's body. What destination did Laura have in mind tonight? Had she planned to be with another man she'd met before? Nothing about her added up. There was only one way to find out the truth. He picked up his clothes and started for his house.

"Do you want to stay and swim with me?"

"I'm afraid I can't right now. I have plans, but we'll do some laps tomorrow."

"Okay."

"À toute à l'heure."

"Ciao."

Once he reached the house Raoul pulled out his cell phone and dialed the limo driver. Pierre picked up on the third ring. *"Oui, Monsieur Raoul?"*

"Where are you now?"

"Villefranche."

"Et Mme Aldridge?"

"She's walking the grounds of the Villa Leopolda."

"How much longer do you expect she'll be?"

"Since she just got started, I would imagine a half hour anyway. Is there an emergency?"

"*Non.* This can wait. *Merci,* Pierre." He clicked off.

CHAPTER FOUR

LAURA was making her way back from the Villa Leopolda estate when she discovered the limo was gone. In its place an unfamiliar black Mercedes sedan stood parked, but a dangerously familiar Frenchman in cream trousers and a soft yellow crew neck lounged against the front fender watching her progress.

After their wild skirmish that had raised more questions than it had answered during the day, there was no escaping Raoul. As a matter of fact, she did wonder if he might come looking for her because he was a man who couldn't tolerate unfinished business. She had thought she'd figured out why he didn't like her, and under the circumstances she had made up her mind to be nicer to him.

Guy's family was very close-knit. While they were going through this terrible period with Chantelle, Raoul obviously resented any outsider coming in. Laura could understand that. With tensions running high it was always harder to behave normally around a stranger. Raoul wasn't used to anyone else being there. Perhaps he was even a little jealous that he didn't have Chantelle's full attention when he did drop in.

Because Laura had half expected to see him before the night was over, her footsteps didn't falter as she made her way toward him. It was only 9:20 p.m., that magic time of night between darkness and light.

He waited with his powerful arms folded. Though a modern man in contemporary clothes, he had the look of a dark, forbidding prince who might have had the estate behind her built for his own private pleasure.

A strange half smile lifted one corner of his

compelling mouth. "If you're in the market for a piece of property, the villa can be purchased if you make an offer over 500 million American dollars."

She stopped three feet from him. "That's what the pilot told me when he flew me over it when I arrived here. I'm afraid I don't earn that kind of money."

"A woman like you doesn't have to."

Another glove slapped against her cheek. And here she'd been feeling more charitable toward him.

"You mean all I have to do is ask *you* to buy it for me and *voilà*—it's mine?"

He straightened to his imposing height, reminding her how incredibly appealing he was. "It might be…for a price."

She nodded. "That's fair. I doubt even King Leopold's first mistress knew he only planned to install her here for a season. She was a fool…like all the others that followed her. What *is* yours? Price, I mean." It gave her a secret thrill to bait him.

His expression hardened, filling her with satisfaction that he couldn't have it all his own way every second. "It might be too high."

"You mean for a woman like me," she mimicked him. "You've made your point and are probably right."

"Stop the pretense, Laura."

She'd had it with him. "What have I done wrong now, Raoul?"

A bleak expression entered his eyes, almost human. She didn't know he could look like that, and it softened her to discover he might have feelings. "According to Pierre, you've been out here two hours. That's a long time when you can't even tour the rooms."

"I wasn't interested in the interior."

"Somehow that doesn't surprise me."

"Since you've already decided what kind of woman I am, I guess it wouldn't."

He sucked in his breath. "What's your real reason for being here?"

She laughed. "My real reason? What's yours?"

His black brows formed a bar above his

eyes. "Paul hoped you'd be back so you'd teach him CPR."

"Paul was very endearing when he said he'd like to learn, but I couldn't pin him down to a time. We decided to play it by ear."

"Are you certified?"

"Yes. Since you're such a protective uncle, I'll have you know I've taught hundreds of people."

"Even adult males?"

She cocked her head. "Are you needing a lesson?"

"And if I were?" he mocked.

She eyed him frankly. "I don't know. Can you afford me? But maybe the better question to ask would be, can your reputation stand being in the company of a married woman like me?"

A little nerve hammered at his temple. "*How* married are you?" he demanded.

If she wasn't mistaken, the subject had him all worked up. This was getting fascinating. "You either are, or you aren't. Which are you, by the way, Raoul?"

"Don't change the subject."

"It's the same subject, as far as I can tell, Raoul. Why don't you want to talk about yourself? What are you afraid of?" she teased with a smile. "Has your wife hired a private detective to follow your every move so he can show her pictures of the latest woman in your life? I'm told blackmail is still big business in France. Especially when you're talking the Laroche fortune. Come on and tell me the truth. Who has more? You or Guy?"

His chest rose and fell visibly. "Does he know what you've been doing out here alone?"

Laura couldn't keep up with his thought processes. He was all over the place. She felt like she was on the witness stand. "Of course. He's the one who suggested I ask Pierre to drive me."

The glitter coming from those dark eyes jolted her. "Guy would do anything for you wouldn't he."

"Well…I did save his life."

"Can you prove it?" he bit out.

"No, but I imagine if you ask any of his friends who were there like Maurice or Luigi, they would be able to tell you. Luigi was exceptionally grateful to me too. In fact, he asked me if I'd like to spend the night at his villa in Rome, but Guy got to me first."

Raoul shifted his weight restlessly before staring into her eyes. "I'll concede I've been a little rough on you. For the last time, why did you come out here to this villa?"

"So if I tell you now, you'll believe me?"

"Let me hear it first," he murmured, though it seemed to cost him to allow even that much latitude.

"I wanted to do some sketches of the estate while there weren't too many people around." I wanted to get away from you. "During the day visitors often stop to talk or ask questions and it interrupts my concentration. Does that satisfy you?"

"No." He almost hissed the word.

The white-hot heat of anger ran up her body

to her face. "That's because you hoped to catch me with a man so you could tell your brother to throw the scheming opportunist out of his house. Before you do that, you'd better be able to explain how I had time to do *this!*"

She opened her tote bag and thrust the sketchpad at him. "Go on. Look inside. I dare you," she whispered because if she said it in any louder, she'd rouse the security people stationed around the villa.

In an economy of movement he turned back the cover. It was a new sketchpad, the one she'd put in her purse before they left for Antibes. The first three pages were drawings she'd done down on the marina while she had been waiting for him. However, the next twenty contained her series of the Villa Leopolda.

Not even Raoul could argue that she'd had time for a secret tryst and still complete that many detailed drawings in a two-hour time limit. This was the first time he'd seen any of her artwork. He studied each one for an indefinite period. She experienced immense delight watching him eat crow.

Eventually he closed it and handed it back to her. His eyes were mere black slits. "You're very gifted," his voice grated.

"But you still dislike me. I can live with that as long as you stay out of my way until the two weeks are up. So far you've had trouble in that department." His lips thinned at that remark. She couldn't be happier. "As you can see from your own experience, men have a hard time leaving me alone, whatever their private reasons. It gets tiring and I'm tired. May I have a ride home, please?"

After a thorough study of her features, he opened the front passenger door for her. She moved past him and got in, thankful she'd worn pants with her striped top. Every time his searching gaze wandered over her, she felt exposed and vulnerable.

Once he closed the door and went around to the driver's side, she slipped the sketchpad into her purse, but when she started to fasten her seat belt he forestalled her and drew her into his arms. The action brought her cheek against his freshly shaved jaw, causing her hair to flounce like gold silk. Sensing he was going to kiss her, she hid her face in his neck.

He bit her earlobe gently. "You know we've both been wanting this since we met. Why so coy, Laura?"

She admitted it, but he'd chosen the wrong word. It had a connotation that meant she was playing a game, pretending to be shy while at the same time being intentionally flirtatious and silly. Though he hadn't meant to, he'd brought her back to reality in a hurry.

She moved her head so she could see into his eyes. "That's right," she mocked. "From a woman like me you want brazen. I'm afraid I'm all out of that flavor today."

His face darkened with lines. "Let's find out, shall we?" He crushed her mouth with his own. Slowly he began devouring her, giving her little chance to breathe with her gathered so closely against him. The primitive nature of the kiss rocked her to the core, calling out her natural desire.

With no other people around, Laura had the sense they were far away from civilization. Alone with this man, she was spinning out of control. It frightened her she could feel this way so fast and she started to pull away.

"I'd say that was an interesting experiment," he murmured against her lips before allowing her to move away from his arms. "It leaves me to wonder if you respond the same way to other men…to my brother for instance."

Her head jerked around. Shock set her back so it was difficult to find the words. Her veins had turned to ice water.

"I knew you had your suspicions about me, Raoul, but do you mean to tell me you've been kissing me, holding me, and all this time you've believed that Guy and I are lovers?"

His features remained impassive. "You have no idea how much I haven't wanted it to be true."

"But there's a part of you that still believes it?"

"Laura—"

"You *do!*"

He shook his head. "I know Guy wants you for comfort. I've seen it with my own eyes."

"Comfort is a far cry from a sexual relationship!"

His eyes had a desolate cast. "They can be two sides of the same coin."

"That's true if you're in love. Guy's in love with Chantelle!"

"She doesn't want him anymore."

"So you assume he's turned to me?" Right now she was so hurt she wanted to die. "I want to go back to the villa. Would that be too much to ask, or shall I just jump out and walk home?"

The tension vibrated between them before he started the motor and pulled out of the parking area onto the main road. He worked with calm precision. His movements automatic. Poetry in motion, but it had the effect of infuriating her more.

The silence on the drive back to Cap Ferrat was louder than any more questions he could throw at her. All the time he'd been vetting her, he refused to satisfy her curiosity about him on a solitary thing.

As he pulled up to the front of the darkened villa she tried to get out, but he'd set the lock. When she glanced over at him, he lay back against the seat seemingly relaxed for the moment, but she wasn't fooled. He could pounce at the slightest provocation.

"Perhaps now that we've both had a chance to cool off," he drawled, "you'll tell me the real reason you accepted my brother's invitation to stay with them."

She bowed her head. "Since you've already been told the first version, perhaps you should be asking your nephew. He was at the Palio and heard Guy ask me to come."

"Paul doesn't have a clue about a woman like you."

"*Merci.*"

His muffled French curse rent the air inside the car. "You know what I was implying."

"I'm not sure I ever know what you really mean and I'm too exhausted to undergo another interrogation."

"That's too bad because I want an answer. Even you have to agree that after one meeting in Siena while you're supposedly working, it was highly irregular for you to come into his home the very next morning and end up being his wife's companion for the next two weeks."

She flung herself around so she was facing him. "You obviously meant 'highly suspect.' I suppose it is…coming from a paranoid, bitterly jaded, twisted mind like yours. It's evident someone scarred you for life, Raoul, that's why I have no intention of answering any more of your questions. It would be pointless. Let me out of the car."

"I'm not through with you yet," he countered, making no move to undo the lock button at the side.

Laura had reached the limits of her tolerance.

"Then let it be on your head." Without thought for the consequences, she reached over with the intention of pressing on the horn so security would come running, but Raoul was too fast for her and caught her in his grasp.

"Let's finish what we started a few minutes ago, shall we? Nighttime means we don't have an audience, so you don't need to worry that I have any other interest than enjoying myself with you."

Once more his mouth descended on hers, stifling any sound of protest she made. With an urgency that seemed part of the need that was driving both of them, he coaxed her lips apart again, provoking a kiss from her she couldn't hold back. Like a match to kindling, the pressure of his mouth, the feel of his hands running up and down her arms set her on fire.

Raoul's sensuality made her feel things she'd never felt in her life. How could she be doing this after only a couple of days of knowing him? This had to stop, but when she tried to ease away from him, he pulled her closer against him and this time the horn did sound loud and long.

The shrill din brought Guy out the front door where the lights from the foyer of the villa illuminated the interior of the Mercedes. Paul was right behind him. On a groan she moved back to her side of the car, but Raoul held on to her wrist and her action wasn't fast enough to escape him. They'd been well and truly caught.

Guy came down the steps to open the door for her, but of course it didn't give. Laura struggled in vain to pull her hand out of Raoul's grasp. To her chagrin he used the button from the control panel to lower her window.

With her left hand still trapped in his, he leaned across her body. The action caused his shoulder to brush against her chest. "Sorry for the noise, Guy. It was an accident. I hope it didn't upset Chantelle."

After a slight pause, "No one was in bed yet. What happened to Pierre?"

"I caught up with him at the Villa Leopolda and told him I'd bring Laura home."

Guy studied Raoul thoughtfully before glancing at Laura. "Were you able to do some drawings?"

"Yes. The light was perfect."

"*Maman* wants to see them. The Villa Leopolda is one of her favorite places. Can I take them to her?" Paul asked.

"Of course. Here." She reached in her bag for the sketchpad and handed it to him. "Let her keep it tonight. I'll get it back from her in the morning."

"I'd like to see them first if you don't mind, Paul." Guy started looking through it. He kept shaking his head before staring at her. "You're not only an angel, you have genius."

His kindness after Raoul's cross-examination brought tears to her eyes. "It's not true, but thank you."

In the awkward silence that followed, Laura was tempted to expose Raoul to his brother, but at the last second she couldn't do it, not in front of Paul. In truth this fight was between the two of them and no one else.

Since Raoul still had hold of her, there was only one thing to do. Let Guy think what he was already thinking, that she and Raoul had been kissing and somehow in the enclosed space they'd honked the horn by accident.

"Paul? I understand you wanted me to start teaching you CPR tonight. Sorry I wasn't around. You name the time and we'll do it."

"Okay. Can my friends learn it, too?"

"Of course."

"Thanks."

Guy smiled at her. "Don't worry about locking up when you come in, Laura. I'll still be awake and will take care of it."

Raoul's hand tightened just enough to prevent her from getting out of the car to join him.

"All right. See you two in the morning."

With sketchpad in hand, Guy followed his son into the house. As soon as he shut the door, Raoul said, "The fact that you didn't say anything to Guy about me means you're willing to put up with almost anything in order to remain here the full two weeks. I'm giving you warning I'll be watching every move you make."

She smiled so he could see it. "Like I said, men have a habit of hanging around me whether their company is welcome or not."

His eyes glittered. "It's that chemical reaction they're after."

"Et tu, Brute?"

"I'd be a liar if I didn't admit it." He kissed the palm of her hand before letting it go. Thanks to Raoul, she discovered her palm was as sensitive to his touch as the rest of her. She heard the click of the lock. Now that he was tired of torturing her, she was free to go, for the moment.

Raoul watched her get out and hurry inside the house before he took off for his own villa. Guy was good at disguising his true feelings, but one thing was clear, Laura was playing at something by not running after Guy to tell him every monstrous thing Raoul had done.

He was guilty of a lot. The more appealing she was to him, the more aggressive he'd become. He wasn't proud of his behavior. He'd never treated a woman this way in his life, not even Danielle at her worst. Something about Laura Adridge had permeated deep into his psyche.

If she really had only met Guy for the first time at the Palio, he could understand the pull on his brother. But he still couldn't fathom the act of bringing her into his home…unless he was trying to make Chantelle jealous so she'd fight for him.

Was that what Guy was doing? With Laura's knowing or unwitting cooperation? Yet he couldn't imagine it because Paul wouldn't understand. No, Raoul could scratch the jealousy theory and was back to square one where he had no answers except one. She hadn't lied about her artwork. Her talent left him speechless.

He let himself in the house and headed for the bathroom where he kept painkiller. He'd developed a headache that throbbed more violently when he thought of what was going on at Guy's.

Chantelle's feelings aside, Raoul hadn't missed the look that had passed between Laura and his brother after he'd complimented her. Those tears shimmering like green gems had brought Guy to his knees. She had him so sewn up, it wouldn't surprise him if he ended up divorcing Chantelle.

Raoul was aghast that he had allowed his own thoughts to get that far. Whatever, he had to believe this problem with Chantelle was temporary. He would never have guessed anything could rock the solidity of their marriage.

Then again, Raoul couldn't have imagined that a woman like Laura existed, let alone that she would show up in Guy's world. She was so beautiful Jean-Luc had gone into ecstatic raves over her. "She's the embodiment of my every fantasy, Raoul. You lucky dog you."

During his walk with her through Tourettes, he'd pretended he didn't mind that every red-blooded male within sight was instantly in love and followed her with his eyes. Men dreamed, but only occasionally did they see a female in the flesh who surpassed those dreams.

A woman like her—maybe married several times and apparently still attached to her latest because she needed money—wouldn't know what it was to be faithful, but enough money might keep her around for a long time. Guy's assets would entice her indefinitely.

With Chantelle constantly keeping him at a distance, his brother was ripe to make a mistake that would tear the entire family apart. Maybe Guy and Laura weren't lovers yet, but Raoul couldn't stand by and watch to see it eventually happen.

And you know why, don't you, Laroche. Because you want her yourself. He grimaced at his own weakness before getting ready for bed. Just as he was about to climb in, his cell phone rang. He reached across the covers to pick it up. When he discovered who it was, he answered the call.

"*Eh bien,* Louis. Tell me what you've got."

"Not much yet, but I did find out one important thing. Her passport lists her name as Laurel Aldridge Stillman."

Stillman!

So she had lied about her name.

"She's twenty-nine. Address is 302 Fair Oaks Drive, Santa Barbara, California. I'll call you if I learn anything else."

"*Merci,* Louis. You do excellent work. *Bon nuit.*"

For Laura to be living in Guy's home as Laura Aldridge, it was evident her marriage was in trouble. Lies had destroyed Raoul's own union. What part did they play in the disintegration of hers?

After hanging up, Raoul leaped off the bed and went into his study. Before he started making phone calls, he'd do a little research first and see if anything came up on the Internet.

He put in her full name. Almost instantly whole pages of Web addresses appeared. He scanned the listings. One stood out—theodorestillman.com.

Raoul clicked to it. There she was, bigger than life and utterly breathtaking, sitting in a raft near a typically blond American male. The article beneath the photo read:

Mr. Theodore M. Stillman, known as Ted to his older brothers in the law firm of Stillman, Stillman and Stillman, of Santa Barbara, sons of Former Congressman William Stillman of Santa Barbara, and the late Governor Richard Stillman of the great State of California, is seen here with his beautiful wife Laurel Aldridge Stillman, formerly of Manhattan Beach, California, as they take time out from their busy schedule to float down the Colorado River. Ted is planning to run for the congressional seat next year once occupied by his father. Donations to his campaign can be made by clicking here.

Adrenaline filled Raoul's system as he looked for a date when the picture had been taken. When he couldn't find it, he clicked to the other sites. For the most part she was shown in a photograph at a lunch or a gala looking more subdued than her husband who was always smiling—like the kind of slick car salesmen Raoul couldn't abide.

One site put up by the Manhattan Beach Police Department drew his interest. It was a picture of her in a simple summer dress standing next to the police chief. Raoul studied her exquisite features. She was beaming.

The article read:

> Chief Jose Garcia presents the Meritorious Service Award to head lifeguard Laura Aldridge for her constant devotion to duty. She holds the record for the most saves in Manhattan Beach in ten years—467 people can be grateful she was on duty the day they found themselves in trouble.

Raoul could hear himself taunting her, "Can you prove it?"

Two mornings later Laura was pulling weeds around the side of the villa when her cell phone rang. Only two people had her new number, her attorney and Cindy.

She checked her watch while pulling off her gardening gloves. Eight-thirty in the morning in Cap Ferrat meant 11:30 p.m. in California. For either of them to phone her this late their time meant something was wrong. She couldn't handle any bad news where Ted was concerned. Please be Cindy, she murmured to herself as she slid the phone from her blouse pocket.

When she saw her friend's name on the caller ID she expelled a sigh of relief and clicked on. "Hey, Cindy. What's going on?"

"Plenty. Guess who just got the landlord to let him into your apartment?"

For once her body didn't break out in a cold sweat. In fact, Laura could jump for joy. "You've just made my day, Cindy."

"You mean you're not upset?"

"I reached that stage months ago. Don't you see? This means Ted's minions lost track of me the day Guy flew me here in his helicopter. I can guarantee he thought my boss was lying to him when he told him I was still in Europe, so he decided to break into my apartment and try and catch me at home."

"Why doesn't he just give up?"

"His pride. No other Stillman has had a divorce. He wants to use me, but it'll never happen. My attorney's going to love hearing this. Ted has ignored the court order. Unless the Stillmans own the judge, Ted's in big trouble."

"I'm glad."

"So am I."

"How's it going with Chantelle? Are you making any progress?"

"I've gotten her to come outside in her wheelchair while I weed. We talk about the history of Provence. She's very knowledgeable. I've learned tons, but I don't see her warming to her husband yet. It kills me because he's always so sweet to her. Today I'm going to ask her if she'll go to lunch with me somewhere exciting, but I'm not holding my breath."

"All things taken into account, you sound happier than I've ever known you to be."

Laura turned on her stomach and stretched out on the grass lining the flowerbed. "Oddly enough, I am. Guy's villa is a Garden of Eden. I'm sitting in the middle of the most gorgeous arrangement of rose beds you've ever seen. Beyond them is the Mediterranean. This morning it's a dazzling blue dotted with sail-boats. The air is so fragrant a good perfumer should market it."

"It sounds divine, and no serpents in sight."

"I didn't say that, Guy has a brother."

"Older or younger?"

"Younger. The dynamo at the Laroche Corporation."

"Handsome?"

Laura closed her eyes, pressing her hot cheek against her arm. "Find a picture of Adonis and add ten years to him. Even then you won't do him justice."

"Good grief—"

"You can say that again."

"Laura—"

"Yes. I'm in lust with him."

Cindy burst into laughter. "How wonderful!"

"It's what I call pleasure-pain. I still haven't found out his marital status and he believes I'm Mata Hari. When we *are* together, it's like a duel. He has a rapier tongue that can slice you into pieces faster than Zorro."

"What?"

"It's a long story. Do you have time?"

"All night."

She rolled back over to feel the full rays of the sun on her face and legs. With her eyes still closed, she told her about the outing to Tourettes Sur Loup and ended with the other night when she'd discovered him waiting for her outside the Villa Leopolda. She hadn't seen him since and had missed their lethal skirmishes a lot more than she was willing to admit.

After she'd told Cindy all her theories about why Raoul had been so cruel, her friend said, "Maybe he's in a bad marriage like you and is frustrated to be attracted to you when he's not free. Since he hasn't chosen to tell you his marital status, why don't you ask Chantelle?"

Laura expelled the breath she'd been holding. "I could, but I don't want her to think I'm here for any reason but to be her friend for a while. She has to learn to trust all over again. If she thinks I have another agenda, it could ruin any ground I've made with her."

"I see your point, so why don't you ask Guy?"

"I don't dare talk to him about his brother for the very same reason. The truth is, he hasn't offered any information. They're a very close-mouthed family—aristocratic, if you know what I mean. I've been learning things on a need-to-know basis only."

"Wouldn't Guy's son be all right to ask?"

"No. He's good friends with his uncle. They share everything. I have no doubt Raoul vets Paul about me. I don't want to give him anything he can use against me. The other night Paul told him I'd gone out in the limo and the next thing I knew, Raoul came to find me."

"Sounds thrilling to me."

"It would have been if I thought Raoul didn't have another agenda, but he does. That's why if I were to ask Paul any questions that didn't have to do with him, it would stir things up. I'm trying to stay out of trouble and mind my own business."

"Your life story is better than the latest vampire novel I'm reading."

At that remark Laura laughed. When it subsided she said, "Raoul would make a gorgeous vampire."

"According to your description, he'd make a gorgeous—"

"Don't say it," Laura broke in. "I can't afford to think it."

"But you have thought it. I can hear it in your voice."

"It's this place, Cindy, it's out of this world."

"Then what are you going to do about Raoul?"

She moved her arm in front of her eyes. "Nothing."

"You mean you're going to let nature take its course."

"That's the way it has to be. Now I've kept you up too late and you need your beauty sleep. I'll be seeing you in about ten days, but I'll call you before then. Take care."

"You, too."

Laura rang off, thinking about everything they'd discussed. As she lay there soaking up the sun, she felt a cloud pass over. That was odd. She hadn't seen any clouds on the horizon this morning. She removed her arm to look up at the sky and let out a slight gasp.

It was Raoul blocking the sun's rays. He was supposed to be at work! Had he heard any of her conversation with Cindy before he'd moved right in front of her? She found herself the object of his piercing black scrutiny. It took her breath.

He looked impossibly striking in a light-gray business suit that molded his hard-muscled body to perfection. After two days' deprivation, to have this kind of reaction to him alarmed her.

She sat up and got to her feet. Her sleeveless pink blouse and white shorts covered her adequately, but when his gaze roved over her she trembled for no reason. “I take it you were looking for me.”

“Chantelle said you were out here somewhere. Next time I can’t find you, I’d better look under a few plants. What has you so fascinated?”

“While I’ve been gardening I found something interesting. I planned to show it to Chantelle, but she was on the phone. Then I had to take a call and forgot about it until just now.”

“Your boss?” Raoul was always quick to make assumptions.

“No, my best friend, Cindy. We live in an eight-plex across the hall from each other. She watches my apartment for me while I’m away on business.” Laura knew what he was thinking and decided to satisfy that insatiable curiosity of his. “It’s big enough to fit into my closet in the guest bedroom.”

His lips twisted into a smile. “But it’s yours.”

"Exactly."

"Where is this thing you found?"

"Oh—it's here! I took it in the house and washed it." She picked it up off the grass and handed it to him. "I think it must have been a pin. There's a little boy's face on it. So precious." Laura suddenly felt a pain as she thought about having a real little boy of her own. He would have Raoul's arresting features. She shook her thoughts away, reminding herself that it was foolish to think such things.

He studied her for an overly long moment before giving it his attention. "Where exactly did you find it?"

"Around the east side of the house near the sundial."

"I'll have to call the university about this. You've just found a Gallo-Romain artifact. Most of them have been discovered on Mont Leuze not far from here. If you found this on the property, there are probably more."

As he lifted his dark head, his eyes shot to

hers. "Lifeguard, artist…now archaeologist. There's no end to your talents, is there?" He handed it back to her.

Was that a trace of levity she heard coming out of his all-male mouth? Too late if it wasn't because he had her smiling. "Did you have breakfast with Chantelle?"

He slid one hand in his jacket pocket. "No. I've just come from an early business meeting. Why do you ask?"

She moistened her lips that had gone dry in the heat. His eyes followed the movement. "I was hoping she'd had a good night. Maybe I can get her to go out to lunch with me today."

"Chantelle won't do that for anyone," he said in a withering tone, "not even for you."

Laura frowned. "I appreciate the encouragement."

He cocked his dark head. "Once again I try to pay you a compliment, but it's always misconstrued. I was attempting to tell you that she likes you. If anyone could get her to step foot off the estate, it would be you." A thread of sincerity ran through his words.

"Thank you for that," she whispered.

"When I asked her if she'd like to get out today, she told me she had a headache. Since I can't prove she doesn't, I have to leave well enough alone."

She smoothed some loose strands from her brow. "If it's this hard on you, imagine how Guy must feel."

His lips tightened to a narrow line. "A wife who no longer desires her husband is the kiss of death to a marriage."

There was such a deep kernel of suffering she heard in his voice just now, Laura felt a wrench for him. He'd been severely wounded by a woman. She was at a loss what to say to comfort him. It was crazy to think that after the hurtful way he'd treated her, she still wanted to.

"Was there a reason you wanted to talk to me?"

"Yes. The son of a close friend of mine is a competitor in the Tour de France this year. I promised I'd watch for him in the stage coming up tomorrow. Since it looks like the American team is going to win the whole thing, I thought you might like to come with me and we'll cheer our countries on."

He had an ulterior reason for inviting her, but she couldn't prevent the burst of excitement spreading through her body. She longed to spend the day with him, doing something with him that was unrelated to the problems at the Laroche villa. Perhaps she would see a more relaxed Raoul, she might even be able to get him to open up about himself some more. And she had always wanted to see the Tour in person.

"We'll leave midafternoon and fly to Alpe d'Huez in the helicopter. It's a little mountain town. I've booked rooms there. Tomorrow we'll be at the summit to see who goes over first, then we'll fly to Bourg d'Oisons at the bottom to watch the winner cross the finish line. If it's possible, I'll introduce you to Alain Garonne."

Those were names associated with cycling she'd heard of for years. "I…I'll have to check with Guy," she stammered, so thrilled at the prospect of going with him her legs shook.

"If you insist," he muttered, his eyes shuttered.

"Since he asked me to be a friend to Chantelle, I don't want him to think I'm taking advantage of his hospitality."

"No. I'm sure you wouldn't want him to think that." Was he being sarcastic again? She couldn't bear it. "He's at the breakfast table with Chantelle if you want to ask him now."

She nodded. Leaving her things where they were, she followed Raoul around the side of the villa. His long strides mesmerized her as much as the male symmetry of his body. When they reached the patio she saw that Paul had also joined his parents.

Raoul reached for some toast, leaving it to Laura to broach the subject. The moment she did his nephew said, "Can I come, too?"

"You have your dental check up this afternoon, Paul," his mother reminded him. She turned her head in Laura's direction. "The Tour de France used to be one of Raoul's passions. I have no doubt he'll bore you with statistics, but if you're a fan, too, then it should be an exciting experience."

Guy nodded his assent, but he seemed dispirited and preoccupied.

Raoul's gaze swerved to hers. "I'll come for you at three o'clock. Pack a jacket. The mountains cool off in the evening."

She couldn't understand the almost triumphant gleam in his eyes before he disappeared.

CHAPTER FIVE

THE girl from downstairs shot Laura an unfriendly glance. She probably wasn't a day over twenty-two. "You lock it from this side. Or not," she added pointedly before her gaze swerved to Raoul once more and remained riveted.

Had Laura ever acted as desperate over an attractive man at that age? She surely hoped not.

Ever since they'd flown to Alpe d'Huez in the French Alps and had arrived at the Auberge Hôtel where the rooms were upstairs in the loft, the girl at the front desk had fallen all over herself to attract Raoul's attention. The village was packed with tourists from many countries gathered for tomorrow's race. An electric excitement filled the air.

Everywhere she and Raoul walked after leaving the helicopter, some female smiled at him, inviting him verbally and with a sultry look to come and party with her and her friends. Though they could see Laura was with him, they considered this event a free-for-all.

Once the girl had left them alone, Raoul carried her overnight bag into her room and set it down on a chair. "As soon as you're ready, we'll find a restaurant and eat."

"Five minutes is all I need."

His veiled eyes took in the pleated tan pants and white cotton sweater she was wearing before they lifted to her face. When he looked at her like that through his sooty lashes, she felt her insides melt. "I'll meet you downstairs in the lobby."

With a nod Laura shut the door behind him, but she had to cling to the handle for support. He didn't have any idea what his physical presence did to her. Was there ever a more gorgeous man born than Raoul? She was certain he'd intended to bring someone else, but that was before Laura had become a guest in his brother's home. Since then, all plans had changed.

Laura decided he saw her as a freeloader who was taking advantage of Guy, something Raoul couldn't forgive her for, so he'd brought her here with him. Anything to get her out of the villa where she'd made herself at home after saving his brother's life. He probably worried she would try to find a way to stay on longer. Even if she denied it, he wouldn't listen.

Clearly it irritated him that she felt comfortable enough to work in the garden as if she was the chatelaine and Chantelle the guest. He mocked everything she did. Once in a while he let up on his baiting for a moment, but she was under no illusion that his opinion of her would ever soften.

Since she couldn't do anything about his mindset where she was concerned, she decided to enjoy this unexpected trip and not let his jibes ruin the pleasure of this experience. Too soon she would have to go back to California. When she returned she would demand the earliest court date possible to be legally free of Ted.

Hopefully he'd done his worst by defying the court and breaking into her apartment. Laura had a witness on this one. Not even his brothers with all their political clout could block the divorce much longer.

Before coming to Europe she hadn't thought beyond simply getting away where she wasn't forced to think about Ted's next ploy to get her to come back to him. However, everything had changed since the Palio. Being Guy's guest had meant she'd dropped from the radar screen, forcing Ted's hand.

It felt so wonderful to be free for a little, but she realized she wanted to be divorced as soon as possible, whatever it took. Though she could lie to herself all she wanted, one truth stood out from all the rest. Meeting Raoul had made her want to speed up the timetable.

Not because she had hopes of any kind of relationship with him. It wasn't possible because, for one thing, he wasn't free. Laura didn't know the specifics, but some woman had a hold on him that had darkened his pysche, blighted his world.

Chantelle had said as much, although she hadn't used those exact words. Since her brother-in-law definitely didn't approve of Laura, her warning hadn't come any too soon. There were times when she felt he despised her. But then there were other times…

The fact that she could respond so strongly to him in a man-woman way in spite of his enmity had taught her there could be a life out there for her. Laura just had to find the right man and she was sure that good men existed. Look at Guy!

There wasn't a finer husband in the world or one more devoted to his wife. First, however, Laura had to be officially divorced, something she intended would take place as soon as she returned to Manhattan Beach.

Pulling the band off her ponytail, she went into the bathroom to brush her hair and arrange it in a loose knot on top of her head. A fresh application of peach-frost lipstick felt good after working in the sun over the past few days. That much exposure had brought out her California tan, something inevitable because of her lifeguarding duties.

A few new lines around her eyes reminded her she wasn't getting any younger. One day in the near future she wouldn't have the stamina for that kind of work anymore. Life was passing. She'd be thirty next month. If she didn't hurry and do something about it, she could miss out on the best part—like a loving husband and a family, a child to call her own. But whenever she thought about the few years left to try to have a baby, she got too emotional. She wouldn't think about that tonight.

Right now a man who had ambivalent feelings toward her was downstairs where more devastating salvos awaited her. She was ready. She had put on her female armor and was prepared for the next skirmish with the enemy, a man she physically desired to the boiling point. Laura hadn't been kidding when she'd admitted the truth to Cindy.

It was the farthest thing from love; in order for that to occur you had to like each other first. You had to develop a relationship based on trust and mutual understanding. There had to be respect and unselfishness. Admiration for the other's accomplishments. Patience for the other's imperfections. Without those qualities, the most torrid affair would burn up in the oxygen with no ashes to prove anything had ever taken place.

Laura went back into the room. Maybe she'd want a wrap later, but the upstairs was still warm from the day's heat. She'd rather not be bothered with anything but her tote bag. After locking the adjoining door and the door into the hall, she headed for the stairway. On the way down, she saw a dark-blond guy coming up with a Team America logo on his pullover. He bore a superficial likeness to Ted.

The color in his cheeks plus the glaze filming his eyes indicated he'd been partying for a while. She'd seen that look at the beach too many times to mistake it for anything else. And of course he just had to put his hand against the wall so she couldn't proceed.

"Hello, hello..." He smiled at her as if he'd just won the lottery. "Am I hallucinating or are you the most beautiful female I ever saw in my life, sweetheart?" He looked her over, not hiding anything he was thinking. She was used to it.

She had two choices. Use a maneuver that would cause him to fall down the stairs, or she could go back to the room until the drunken oaf was no longer in the hall.

Then to her surprise she didn't have to make either choice because Raoul had come up behind him and put him in an arm lock with a mastery that made her shiver. "Go on down to the foyer, Laura. I'll join you in a minute."

Laura didn't stay to hear any more. The guy was big, but he was no match for Raoul. She'd barely made it to the front desk when he joined her.

"Are you all right?"

She laughed gently, unable to suppress it, now that the irony of the situation had struck her. This was the first time he'd ever shown true concern for her welfare, but he couldn't know that the only moments she'd felt threatened in Europe had been with him.

By his frown he was waiting impatiently for an explanation.

Her eyes searched his. "If you could have seen the look of fury on his face when you pulled a half nelson on him, you'd understand why I found it so amusing. Thank you."

He didn't smile. "How many times a day does this happen to you?"

Not that again— "Dozens! But as you can see, I've survived so far."

"If I didn't know better," he said in a thick tone, "I'd think you were hiding out at Guy's for protection."

She looked away. Her only purpose for being there was because of Guy's invitation, not to elude Ted, that had just been an added advantage. But this conversation was getting too close to certain truths. Though she and Guy had an understanding that she would try to help Chantelle open up and face her fear, he wasn't forcing Laura to stay.

Naturally she could leave anytime she wanted, but then she'd miss out on these infuriating little moments with his brother that thrilled and tantalized her, forcing her to come back for more. Better to let him go on thinking the worst about her. "Can you offer a better place?"

"Let's eat and we'll talk about it."

That sounded vaguely ominous. Maybe he was on an errand for Chantelle and had brought Laura to Alpe d'Huez to tell her she wasn't wanted at Guy's. Perhaps Chantelle hoped she'd be gone by tomorrow and had been the one to suggest Raoul bring her to see the Tour de France, making it sound as if it were his idea.

It hurt to think Chantelle might have been the

reason behind this whole outing. She'd always loved her and wanted more than anything to help her overcome her problem since the accident.

Was everyone in the Laroche household playing a part, even Guy, who'd known from the beginning this experiment would never work and was in denial? She didn't include Paul. He was too young and innocent.

When they stepped outside the hotel, she realized night came early to the mountains, yet everywhere she looked people were milling around. Lots of partying was going on. She saw lovers with their arms flung around each other.

It was the kind of summer ambience that brought back a rush of nostalgia for something she couldn't name. Dreams still not fulfilled? The hope of youth long since past? Whatever it was, she felt an ache made worse because of the aloof male whose very existence filled her body with a painful hunger. Not that she could do anything about those feelings.

She didn't like Raoul, either. Most of the time

he infuriated her. It was very unfortunate that although he resented and insulted her, he was able to ignite her senses at the same time.

He turned his dark head toward her. In jeans and a light-gray Polo shirt, he looked sensational. “What do you feel like?”

In case he thought she expected dinner at a five star restaurant while she sponged off him, she glanced at the café across the street. “Coke and pizza?”

“You can have that anytime.”

“After the crab salad I had for lunch, I’m not that hungry, but we can go wherever you want.”

He gave an unconscious shrug of his broad shoulders. “Pizza’s fine.”

The place was filled with a noisy crowd and people dancing. They had to wait for a bistro table. To converse was almost impossible with the loud music. It wasn’t bad pizza but they served the Pepsi without ice and it tasted awful. All in all she’d made the wrong choice.

When she happened to look at him, his mouth

broke into a white smile that transformed him, causing her heart to skip a beat.

"You *knew* how bad this would be!" She tossed a wadded paper napkin at him. To her amazement he caught it. "I only picked this place bec—"

"Because you were trying to prove you're someone other than who you are," he cut her off smoothly.

With a few hurtful words he'd destroyed a golden moment. The demons Chantelle had talked about were too much for Laura. "I'm glad you know me so well. Under the circumstances you won't mind if I leave you to pay the bill."

She stood up to get away from him, but he prevented her from leaving. "Where do you think you're going?" His dark gaze challenged her. "I happen to know you deserve better than this place or the Auberge."

Laura felt as if she'd suddenly been caught after being pushed off a high castle wall. She simply didn't understand him. He blew hot and cold so fast she couldn't keep up with him.

"We haven't danced since the pool," he reminded her. "You have to admit it didn't last long enough." His thumb caressed her palm, causing her body to go weak. Her heart pounded too hard to be good for her.

"I admit it," she whispered. When Raoul was like this, Laura couldn't think why she should be keeping him at a distance. For once she didn't feel like fighting him. She couldn't, not when he'd just pulled her into his strong arms. "I haven't danced for so long, I've forgotten how."

"Then we'll do what everyone else is doing and simply move in time to the music," he murmured against her lips.

With their bodies so entwined there was no air between them. His mouth was a temptation she couldn't resist and didn't want to. They slowly began savoring each other while they swayed to the music. Their bodies fit perfectly together. She felt as though they were one throbbing entity floating above the world. As the songs changed, so did the intensity of each kiss.

"Raoul," she gasped softly, from needs that caused her to ache.

"Deny it all you want, but it's been like this with us from the start," came his husky response against her neck.

While she clung to him in the middle of the chaos going on around them, she heard some American say, "It looks like those two need a room."

Quick to respond, Raoul whispered against her ear, "Aren't we fortunate it's only across the street. Come on. Let's get out of here."

He put some bills on their table and guided them out of the bar. It had grown more crowded since they'd come in, but she hadn't noticed. At the moment Raoul was her whole world. Laura couldn't get alone with him fast enough.

She held on to him as they made their way back to the Auberge. The depth of her euphoria had caused her to be careless. Ted's minions could be taking pictures, but suddenly it didn't matter to her. Raoul, too, seemed heedless of those things that had been haunting him, making him so cruel to her earlier. Now all that had gone. Nothing registered except this sweet, unexplored heat building between them.

Once Raoul had let them into his room, he picked her up and carried her to the bed. She pulled him down beside her. In the dim light of one small lamp, his hair and skin, his features took on the cast of a dark prince whose black eyes burned with desire for her.

Before she gave in to the clamoring of her senses, she needed an answer to one question. "I haven't asked before now because I didn't think you and I would—" She hesitated, then started again. "I didn't think we'd—"

"—become lovers?" He finished the thought in a silken voice.

Her face went hot. "Yes. I know so little about you. Are you single? Divorced? You've never said."

He followed the line of her eyebrow with his

thumb. "You really don't know? Even after living in Guy's home?"

"No," she answered honestly. "The subject has never come up."

"Why didn't you ask me if I was married?"

She groaned inwardly. "I didn't think it was necessary."

"Why?"

"Because I don't believe you would be here with me like this if you were married. Despite the way you've treated me at times, my instincts tell me you're an honorable man."

His eyes grew veiled. "I've been divorced from my wife, Danielle, for a year, if that's what you mean, but it doesn't necessarily prove me to be honorable. Otherwise I wouldn't be on the verge of making love to Mrs. Theodore Stillman would I?"

The enchantment of the night splintered into a thousand pieces.

Laura could move fast when she had to. Her job at the beach demanded it. She rolled off the other side of the bed and flew out his door with her tote bag. Within seconds she'd locked herself in the adjoining room. It didn't take him long to knock on the door separating them.

"Open up, Laura," sounded his deep voice. "It's time for us to have a serious talk, I think."

At this point she felt sick to her stomach and was so upset she was shaking. How long had he known her real name?

"Why didn't you say you'd been in contact with my husband?"

"Not contact. I had you investigated."

She threw her head back, absolutely stunned. "Why?"

"To protect my family."

Her body shuddered. All along he'd seen her as a threat. "Finally some honesty from you Raoul. My father-in-law already had me thoroughly investigated before he allowed his son to marry me. You and he have a lot in common. I guess that's what comes from having money and power for so many generations you've forgotten the human element.

"If you love Guy, I advise you not to tell him what you've done because in the end, it might come back to hurt you. He's the kindest, most wonderful human being I know and in case you haven't realized it yet, he loves you dearly. Good night, Raoul."

Raoul passed a hand over his face. Was every woman a liar?

For the past little while he could have sworn the two of them were feeling something deep and real between them. Yet all Laura Stillman could think about was Guy.

His poor, beguiled brother was in love with a very married woman who had a wife's access to her husband's fortune. Louis had done his homework. That Fair Oaks address had the same kind of exclusivity as many of the places near Cap Ferrat.

What was she doing in Europe picking up rich

men using her maiden name? She had a successful millionaire husband of her own in tow with looks like a younger Robert Redford. The woman obviously had no shame.

While he stood there trying to blot pictures of Laura and her husband making love from his mind, the hotel phone rang. Raoul grimaced. After being found out, she was too petrified to face him, so she'd resorted to the phone.

With his emotions exploding all over the place he walked to the bedside table and grabbed the receiver. Fighting for calm he answered, "Laura?"

"Who's Laura?"

Danielle—

Another one of her desperate, attention-seeking phone calls. Perfect timing.

"Don't hang up on me yet, *mon amour.* I remember a passionate night we once spent at the Citadel in Alpe d'Huez during the Tour de France. I thought you might be there for this year's race. When they said you weren't registered, I called several other places.

"What are you doing at the Auberge? Slumming with the riffraff doesn't sound like you. Do you have any idea how much I miss you? I know I was wrong for what I did, but how can you throw away what we once had?"

"It's too late, Danielle."

"Of course it isn't. Oh, Raoul, I love you still so much." She pleaded. "Please let me show you how it can be again. Give us a second chance—"

For a moment he heard the old Danielle in her voice, but her repentant plea still didn't move him. Five days ago something had happened to Raoul that had turned him into a different man. Someone new had entered the picture....

He glanced at the door to the adjoining room, his pulse pounding while he waited for Laura to make a move.

"It's too late." Far too late. "*Adieu,* Danielle," he murmured.

Raoul put the phone back on the hook, smothering her angry shout. Before she could call him again, he turned off the ringer.

He could go down to the bar, but no amount of alcohol would wipe out the sting of Laura's lie. Even though her betrayal was against her husband and his brother, Raoul was the one reeling.

Laura cried so hard all night that when morning came, her eyes were swollen shut. When she left the room at 7:30 a.m. with her overnight bag, she was forced to cover them with her sunglasses.

She hadn't seen or talked to Raoul since he'd dropped his bombshell outside the door last night. Because he'd brought her here to suit his no-longer-secret agenda, she didn't feel obligated to discuss anything more with him. She'd see the day through and tough it out, but that was it. When they returned to Cap Ferrat, she'd stay out of Raoul's way until she returned to the States.

The Auberge served a continental breakfast in the dining area off the foyer. Only a few people were eating. The rest had left to line the road while they waited for the bikers making the ascent. After choosing a baguette and some juice, she sat down at a table. Though she had no appetite, she knew she'd better eat something.

While she munched on the bread without enthusiasm, Raoul entered the dining room wearing his jeans and a navy sport shirt, unbuttoned at the neck where she could see a smattering of dark hair. She closed her eyes tightly to shut off the view, but it was too late to stop the warm rush that permeated her weakened body.

He reached for her bag and took both of them to the counter in the lobby to be held until later. Afterward he wandered over to the side bar for a cup of coffee and a baguette. When he returned, he took the seat opposite her and dunked his bread in the hot liquid before eating it with obvious enjoyment. There was clearly no problem with his appetite.

"When you're ready, we'll walk over to the road and watch what we came to see." His voice sounded half an octave lower this morning. Even after everything that had transpired, she still ached for him.

There was a tiny cut at the side of his jaw where he must have hurt himself shaving. It was the only thing she could find that might indicate he wasn't in total control. Somehow the thought was reassuring.

As she was finishing the last of her juice, he lifted her sunglasses from her face. His knuckle brushed the end of her nose. "I thought so," he muttered before setting them back in place.

She froze. "You're a true Frenchman all right. When you butcher your animal, you don't leave any parts."

A faint white line of anger circled his mouth. Good.

He got up from the table at the same time she did. Like a couple who'd lived too long together and didn't find pleasure in each other's company, they left the hotel with several feet between them and made their way down the side street to the main road packed with fans. It was tragic, really, that she couldn't enjoy the glorious view from this famous spot, but she was too numb.

Raoul found a place where they could stand and see everything. She people watched in order not to stare at him. They were probably the only two fans on the mountain who weren't chatting excitedly. After twenty minutes the first cars riding ahead of the bikers came in sight. The crowd grew noisier. Pretty soon there was an explosion of sound because the first five racers had been spotted.

They looked hot and miserable. Deep lines around their mouths reflected the strain on their bodies. Everyone passed them cups of water. Sometimes the passage became so narrow she was afraid a tourist would ruin the race for them. Finally they cycled in front of her and Raoul. None of the five were on the French or American teams.

A few minutes after they started down the other side of the summit, up came the peloton. For a second she spotted the biker in the yellow jersey. The whole scene looked chaotic when you were seeing it in person rather than on TV.

The cyclists rode past, their legs moving like pistons. Several of them fell back, their bikes moving wobbily, as if the racers were on the verge of collapse.

All this effort to see them go by. Now it was over.

She glanced at Raoul through her sunglasses. “I’m going to walk to the helipad.”

He nodded. “I’ll be there as soon as I collect our luggage.”

Without watching him, she took off down the mountain at a brisk pace. It felt good to expend some energy. This was one time when she wished she could plunge in the surf and swim way out to catch a wave.

Amazing that by the time she reached the helicopter, Raoul had somehow caught up to her and showed no signs of being winded. She greeted the pilot, then climbed in the back and strapped herself in.

Raoul stowed their bags, then took his place in the copilot’s seat. He spoke in rapid French to the pilot before the blades began to rotate.

Once they were whipping the air, the helicopter lifted off, leaving her stomach behind.

The scene out the window could only be described as spectacular. She could see the zigzag road beneath them, but there was no sign of the cyclists because the helicopter was headed in the opposite direction from Bourg d'Oisons, the end of the day's eighth stage.

She didn't need to ask Raoul anything. He'd accomplished what he had come here to do, but since she hadn't given him the satisfaction of an explanation, he was taking her home, thank heaven.

While Raoul and the pilot talked quietly together, the uneventful flight back to Cap Ferrat allowed her to sleep. When she woke up, she was surprised to discover they'd landed on the estate.

Raoul had already climbed out of the helicopter and had put her bag in the limo. "Pierre will take you to the villa."

She said a collective thank-you to him and the

pilot before getting in the car. Raoul shut the door as if he couldn't wait to see her gone from here. Nothing could hurt more than the memory of last night when she'd thought Raoul had truly started to care for her. To think all along he'd been waiting for the perfect moment to expose her. The pain of it was excruciating.

After reaching the villa, Pierre got out and handed her the overnight bag. She thanked him before hurrying inside the house. She almost ran into Guy, who must have heard the helicopter and was coming out to greet her.

He gave her a hug before looking at her. "What's wrong?" he asked immediately. "You look pale. Did the helicopter make you ill?"

"Oh, no. I'm a little tired." She put her bag down.

"You're back sooner than I would have expected."

"As it turned out, Raoul didn't want to see the end of the stage because his team wasn't winning." A white lie, but it was the best she could come up with at the moment. He smiled.

"My brother always was a terrible loser. Now you've seen him at his worst."

Guy could have no idea…. "How's Chantelle?"

A shadow crossed over his features. "She went down for a nap a little while ago."

"And Paul?"

"With a friend. They've gone bike riding."

"Guy—" She took a huge breath. "Could we talk in private?"

"*Bien sur.*"

"But if you were working—"

"It's nothing I can't do later. Let's go to your sitting room. No one will disturb us there." That's right. It was the one room in the villa off-limits to Raoul.

He carried her bag down the hall for her. She went inside the suite first. After he followed her in, she shut the door and they both sat down on the chairs placed around the coffee table.

"Guy—there's something vitally important I have to tell you."

"I already know."

She blinked. “Know what?”

“About you and Raoul.”

Laura started to feel sick again. “There is no me and Raoul, Guy.” Her heart was thudding too fast for it to be healthy.

“Jean-Luc seems to think so. He called me this morning. He doesn’t want to lose out on this latest sale in Antibes. Since Raoul won’t commit yet, he’s been trying to convince me the property is worth buying. That’s when it all came out. He saw you in front of the warehouse with my brother.”

Laura sat forward in a panic, her thoughts reeling. “If you’re talking about that kiss, Raoul did it as a joke. Chantelle told me he has his little demons. I think one came out that day.”

Guy chuckled. “My brother has been full of surprises lately.”

“He’s very amusing. I know it didn’t mean anything. He said the real estate agent was a huge gossip, and he wagered you’d hear about it within twenty-four hours. Looks like he was right.

"Seriously though, you've all been terrific to me including Raoul, who's been kind enough to show me around. He made it possible for me to see a stage of the Tour de France. I was thrilled."

He nodded. "I'm glad you're having a good time."

She eyed him soulfully. "I am, but we both know that's not why I'm here. I wish I could say I was having a lot of success with Chantelle."

"While you've been here, I've seen a change in her. You've brought new life into the house. Don't give up on her."

"Of course I won't, but there's one more thing I'm worried about. My husband has the resources to try to find me while I'm here. I just want you to be aware of it. You need to know his name is Theodore Stillman. He's an attorney from Santa Barbara, California, with enough backing from his family to cause trouble if he wants. If there's the slightest problem that could upset Chantelle, I'll leave here."

Guy's mouth firmed before he stood up. "Don't you worry. I have my own attorneys who can deal with anything the Stillman attorneys might concoct."

Laura didn't doubt it.

"Do you want cook to fix you a late lunch?"

"No, thank you. I think I'll rest for an hour. Maybe by then Chantelle will be up and I'll tell her about the race."

"She'll love that. See you later."

As he leaned forward to give her a kiss on both cheeks, she heard Raoul's rasping voice in the periphery. "The maid said I'd find you in here, *mon frère.*" He moved deeper into the sitting room. His glittery gaze fell on Laura.

"I did knock, but you didn't hear me. Sorry to disturb, but Paul has had a mishap on his bike coming home from his friend's. An ambulance took him to the hospital to check him out. The E.R. called to say he's fine. They're ready to release him to his parents."

"He's all right?" Guy looked visibly shaken. Raoul nodded. *"Grâce a ciel!"*

"Do you want me to get him?" Raoul asked. "If he's here before Chantelle wakes up, then she won't be as disturbed when he tells her what happened."

"Let's both go, Raoul." He turned to Laura. "Will you stay here? If Chantelle wakes up before we're back, tell her we went on an errand."

"I will, but, Guy? Maybe she should be told. Paul's her son, too. She adores him. If she thought he needed her, she might forget herself for a little while and go with you. You never know."

His eyes grew suspiciously bright. "Why didn't I think of that? *Dieu merci* you're here, Laura! I'm going to wake her up right now. Things couldn't be any worse than they have been. Why not act on your suggestion and see what happens?" He kissed her cheek again before dashing out of the suite.

CHAPTER SIX

LAURA stood there trembling. "If you don't mind, I'd like to be alone."

"What if I *do* mind?" Raoul challenged. His brother had gone. "Did you tell him I had you investigated?"

Her eyes looked wounded. "I don't know why you bother to ask me, when we both know you don't believe a word that comes out of my mouth."

He raked a hand through his hair. "That's not true, Laura."

"I thought you would want to go with your brother. He needs you."

"I think I'll wait a few minutes. You gave him an idea. Coupled with his guilt over the accident, he might achieve a little success with Chantelle."

When she bit her lip like that, her whole persona changed from the confident woman of the world to someone sweet and vulnerable. Which one was she, or was she an amalgamation of both?

"Once before, you mentioned Guy's guilt about the accident. Why should he feel any blame?"

Raoul rubbed his chest absently. "Apparently they'd had an argument that day, one of the few in their marriage. Chantelle was all set to visit a good friend of hers who lives in Monaco. Guy is superstitious about certain things and he told Chantelle he didn't want her to drive the Monaco road, because it was too dangerous. Princess Grace died on that road.

"She refused to listen to him on that subject. On that particular day he forbade her to go, but she went anyway and ended up having the accident. Not on that road, as it happens, not even in Monaco. It took place in Nice. She was driving her sports car too fast. It shimmied on a bridge. She lost control and it rolled into some heavy shrubbery where the car lay hidden for four hours."

Laura sank down on the nearest chair. "How ghastly."

"It was, for a lot of reasons. Guy took it all on, saying it was his fault he'd upset her, thus the reason she'd gone over the side. When the doctor told her she was fully recovered and could stop using the wheelchair, she reverted to the way she is today.

"At first Guy thought she was teasing to get back at him, but after twelve hours it became apparent something much more serious was preventing her from returning to normal. Needless to say, he's been going downhill ever since, as has their marriage."

A gasp escaped her throat. "All they need is this bad news about Paul." She covered her eyes with her hand. "How serious are his injuries?" she whispered.

"A gash on the side of his left thigh. It took ten stitches."

"Ouch."

"He'll be fine."

"Was it his fault?"

"No. A truck passed another car and drifted into the bike lane, sending Paul flying."

"That must have been so frightening for him." She jumped back up from the chair, obviously too restless to sit. "Your family can't take much more."

Raoul studied her well-shaped head, marveling at the color of her pale-blond hair. It had an ethereal quality, all the more stunning on such a striking woman. Today she wore it loose from a side part. Of all the styles, he liked it the best.

"I couldn't agree more." He moved closer to her. "My brother is more fragile than you know. Whatever goes on between you and your husband is your own business, but if it could hurt Guy, then it becomes *mine.* Why are you afraid to talk about your husband?" he asked her in a voice she had never heard from him before: soft, gentle.

A nervous hand went to her throat. “Why haven’t you ever talked about your wife?”

Her response exasperated him. “Because this is about Chantelle and Guy, not me. Are you in some kind of trouble?”

“That depends on your definition of the word.”

“You mean Guy’s going to help you.”

She flashed him a warning glance. “I’m afraid that’s none of *your* business. Unlike you, I meant no offense. In case you didn’t notice, I don’t ask you personal questions.”

“I’ve noticed,” he said sharply, growing more frustrated every second. “What would you like to know?”

He watched her swallow, another telltale sign she was growing more and more uncomfortable. “Nothing.”

Such an innocuous word said so innocuously. “Surely you’ve wondered why I don’t seem to have a household of my own.”

“Not really.”

“That’s a lie.”

She folded her arms against her shapely waist. "Since you're now reverting to your baser instincts, I guess that's my cue to ask the ten-million-dollar question."

He smiled wickedly and her insides lit. "It's nice to know you put that high a price on the answer."

She tossed her head, causing her hair to float above her shoulders. "All right, I give up. Why did you and your wife divorce?"

"She lied to me about something I can never forgive her for. All the time we were married I thought she wanted children as much as I did. We planned to have a family, but she never had any intention of getting pregnant."

Something flickered in the depths of those green orbs. "She did a very cruel thing to you. I'm sorry."

"Aren't you going to ask me anything else?" he prodded.

"I don't need to. A lie says it all, don't you think?"

If he didn't miss his guess, that was pain he

heard in her voice. "Not all. The follow-up might be. Am I sad about my marriage being over? Am I happy it came to an end?"

Her expression closed. "If you're sad, then it's a tragedy. If you're happy, then it speaks for itself."

"What about *your* marriage?" he drilled her, ready to erupt if she didn't tell him something he could understand.

"You mean am I in a state of bliss, or some-place lower?"

A tight band constricted his breathing. "I think the fact that you're living under Guy's roof says a lot."

"There you go, then." She smiled. "You have your answer."

His hands shot to her shoulders. He shook her almost roughly. "Don't do this, Laura. I'm not asking you these questions out of some twisted desire to torment you. Has your husband been abusive to you?"

She averted her eyes. "Not physically."

"But there are other ways."

"That's true, but I don't wish to discuss it, Raoul." Her breathing had grown shallow. "How long have you known my married name was Stillman?"

"Not long."

Her eyes filled. "Then why didn't you confront me immediately instead of plunging in the dagger last night?"

He'd only meant to get the truth about her feelings for her husband out in the open, but things were fast escalating out of control. He found himself kneading her upper arms not covered by her blouse. His thumbs smoothed her skin with its golden glow. Her body was warm and fluid. Fragrant.

"Last night still haunts me, so I'll ask it another way. Is fear of your husband the reason you've sought Guy's help?"

Her lips were only inches apart from his. "After the history between us, why would it possibly matter to you?"

"Because you're a married woman, and I need to kiss you again or go slowly out of my mind."

She quivered against him. He felt her warm, sweet breath on his lips as she said, "You've already done that on several occasions."

"Not like this…"

With his conscience nowhere in sight, he covered her mouth hungrily. She'd been a temptation since he'd first seen her in Guy's living room enamoring all his male guests.

"We mustn't—" she cried, refusing him entry. Not to be defeated, he kissed his way around her lips, finding every line and curve, lingering on the fuller parts. That brought another small gasp, giving him the entrée he craved. He slid his hands over her back and pulled her into him so he could drink deeply.

She was ready for him, just like last night. Her little moans closed any escape hatch he should have been looking for. Slowly covering every inch of skin, his mouth moved to her throat where the pulse at the base throbbed wildly.

Raoul thought he'd known rapture before, but never like this. "You're so beautiful, Laura. I ache whenever I think about you, let alone look. I want you."

She reached up to cup his face before pressing a lingering kiss to his lips. "There's nothing like it, is there? A fire that burns so hotly you think you can't live without it." Her eyes burned with that fire. "But somehow we do." One more short kiss and she eased out of his arms.

"*We* don't have to live without it," he murmured huskily.

"Yes *we* do." She'd already backed away emotionally from him. "Our lives were going in two different directions when we collided. The chemistry's real, Raoul, but that's all. I'm still Mrs. Stillman, and I'm here at Guy's request to try to help Chantelle."

He felt as if his air supply had just been caught off. "Have you considered that Chantelle might see you as a threat?"

The way she looked at him, he might as well

have slapped her. She studied him for a long time. "Your divorce has given you such a cynical view of life, you don't know what's real anymore. It's sad because you're truly a wonderful person in so many ways.

"Over the last few days there've been slices of moments of sheer pleasure with you. I thank you for those, but Chantelle gave me some good advice on my first day here and I quote, 'Don't let him scare you off, Laura. Raoul has his own demons he needs to deal with. Guy brought you to our home at my request. Raoul has his own home. Your being here is none of his business.'"

She walked to the door of the suite. "You look exhausted. You'd better go home and get some sleep, otherwise someone else I know is going to end up in the hospital before the day is out. I'll phone you if there's any kind of development."

His eyes probed hers. "I could use a few hours, but I'll be back. Care to join me?" he asked, smiling wickedly.

Her heart thudded in her chest. "If that's a proposition, it's not a flattering one. You're half-dead."

"You want me fully alive, is that what you're saying?"

Her breath caught. He might be exhausted, but the wicked smile was in evidence. "I'm saying the timing is wrong, even for chemistry. You know the expression 'There's a time to weep and a time to laugh…a time to mourn and a time to dance'?"

"And now isn't the right time for us?" he murmured. Laura nodded. "It's your loss, Laura. I think there is more than just chemistry between us."

Laura couldn't take any more. Since he made no move to leave she said, "You're welcome to stay in here and sleep. I'm going to find out whether Guy was successful in getting Chantelle to go to the hospital with him. When Paul comes home, I'll send the maid to let you know."

Raoul felt like he'd just awakened to a nightmare.

* * *

The sound of a car in the drive had Laura putting down her sketchpad to dash to the front door. When she opened it, the sight of three people getting out of the limo brought tears to her throat. Chantelle had gone to the hospital with Guy to bring their son home. Another big step for her.

Dear Guy. He had double duty. After he and Pierre lifted Chantelle and her wheelchair to the top step of the porch, he rushed back to help Paul with his crutches. One pant leg had been rolled up high enough to expose a patch of gauze and a bandage covering his wound.

Knowing Chantelle wouldn't want Laura to say anything about this minor miracle of her going to the hospital, she focused on her son.

"Hey, Paul, maybe we should have taken you with us to see the Tour after all," she called out.

He looked up at her with a wan smile. "How was it?"

"Not nearly as hair raising as what happened to you. Is your bike ruined?"

"Yeah."

"I'm sorry. A bike can be replaced, but there's only one Paul Laroche."

"Will you be my nurse?"

Laura smiled and gave him a kiss on the cheek. "I insist on it." Her gaze switched to Guy, who winked at her. He looked happier than she'd seen him since her arrival in Cap Ferrat. Today had been a milestone, not only for Chantelle.

She wheeled through the foyer. "We're very thankful to bring you home in one piece, *mon fils*. Let's get you to your room."

"Do I have to go to bed, *Maman?* I want to lie on the lounger out on the patio."

"You're sure it's not too hot for you?"

"I'll arrange the umbrella for him," Laura offered.

Everyone moved through the house to the patio off the dining room. "Has the medicine made you sick?" his mother asked.

"No. I'm hungry."

Chantelle looked at him with loving eyes. "You've a cast-iron stomach just like your uncle."

"Did I hear my name taken in vain?"

Raoul's head and shoulders had emerged from the pool. He must have slipped out the front door after Laura had left the guest suite. Had he gotten any sleep?

With enviable male grace he levered himself out of the water and onto the tile. In a few strides he reached his nephew and laid the crutches at the side of the lounger so Paul could settle back. Then he tousled his hair. "It looks like you're going to live. Just don't do that again."

Laura's eyes closed. She was still throbbing from the touch of Raoul's hands moving over her back and arms earlier with an urgency that had left her breathless.

"It was the truck driver's fault."

Guy came out with a glass of lemonade for him.

"Merci, Papa."

"I'm going into the house to talk to cook," Chantelle said. "Giles called and wants to know how you are."

"I'll call him later. He was ahead of me and luckily didn't get hit."

Laura hunkered down at his side. "He was lucky, but you carry the mark of bravery."

A smile broke out on his attractive face. One day he was going to be a heart breaker like the rest of the men in the Laroche family. "Yeah."

"Yeah."

"Who won the race?"

"The Dutchman came in first," Raoul informed him. "Places two and three went to the Spanish," he added while he and Guy pulled up chairs next to him. "Not a Frenchman among them."

Paul frowned. *"Zut alors!"*

"Not an American, either," Laura interjected, having pulled up another chair. Paul hooted.

For the next half hour she listened as Raoul gave them details of what they'd seen earlier in the day. Part was in English for her benefit, but a lot of it was in French. She knew he was knowledgeable, but she had no idea he could rattle off names and statistics like a pro announcer, let alone recall everything while she'd been standing there in monstrous pain.

If ever she needed proof that a man could compartmentalize his interests from his emotions, this was it.

Late afternoon turned into evening. Chantelle put a puzzle together with Laura while Paul introduced her to some of his favorite teen rock music. Raoul and Guy discussed a little business. After dinner he convinced his son to go to bed. Tomorrow he could have his friends over.

When Raoul said good-night to everyone and took himself off to his villa, Laura felt a loss she could hardly bear. As upset as she'd been over his admission that he'd had her investigated, his concern that Ted had abused her took away a lot of her pain.

She'd give anything to follow him so they could talk more. So far she hadn't been inside his villa, nor was she likely to be invited. If he'd lived there throughout his marriage she would have no idea, but she felt a deep curiosity over what he did away from his family.

A man like Raoul wouldn't have been celibate since his divorce. If he had a lover, he'd been sandwiching her in since he'd taken it upon himself to keep an eye on Laura. Last night at the Auberge she'd come close to giving him everything. *Oh, Raoul.*

After a sleepless night, Raoul pulled on his swimming trunks. He had a plan in mind to get Laura to himself. That meant spending a little time with Paul at the pool.

Sure enough his nephew dressed in shorts and a T-shirt was already stretched out on a lounger. His leg had been propped. Raoul dived in the water. When he came out the other end, Paul smiled at him. "*Bonjour, mon oncle.*"

"*Bonjour, mon gamin.* Have you had breakfast yet?"

"Yes. I ate out here with Laura."

They'd been up early. "Where's your nurse now?"

"She's bringing me some things from my bedroom."

"Have you made plans with your friends yet?"

"Nope."

"How would you and Giles like to go boating with me and Laura today?"

"Cool!" he cried. "She didn't tell me."

"It's my surprise."

"Hey, Laura," he called to her as she walked out on the patio carrying some things in her arms. Dressed in her white swimsuit with a French braid fastened to the top of her blond head and those long legs going on forever, she looked so beautiful Raoul almost fell back in the pool. "Uncle Raoul is going to take us out on the cruiser! He said Giles could come with us!"

Other than her eyes turning a more brilliant shade of green, she didn't react or make up some excuse why they couldn't go. "As long as it's okay with your parents, I don't see why you shouldn't enjoy a lovely day like this on the water."

She bent over him. "Here's your Ipod, your Game Boy, some sunscreen and the album."

"Thanks."

"You're welcome."

"How about something for me?" Raoul asked, drawing her attention.

"Breakfast coming right up." She disappeared before he could stop her.

Paul started poring over a picture album. "Hey, Uncle Raoul? Do you want to see something cool?"

He pulled a chair up by the lounger. "What is it?"

"Some pictures of me and Laura."

"*Bien sur.*" Giles must have taken them.

"*Maman* found them for me last night before I went to bed."

Found them?

Paul handed over the album. He had it opened to a page with a dozen small photos. They were snapshots, the kind printed years ago. Consumed by curiosity, he studied them.

To his shock he saw Laura in a swimsuit much like the one she was wearing now, but she was a teenager! His mind reeled. The little dark-haired boy she was holding was Paul! In another picture she was dressed in shorts and a blouse while she helped him walk. Still others showed them with Guy and Chantelle on the surf or around a pool.

The blood hammered at his temples. Absolutely stunned, he lifted his head. "Where were these taken, Paul?"

"At thc Manhattan Beach Resort Hotel in California," Laura answered for him. She put the breakfast tray on the little table next to Raoul. "The last summer before I started university, I was a part-time lifeguard and babysitter there." Her gaze flicked to Paul.

"The manager asked me if I would do a special favor and become the Laroches' nanny for the ten days they were there at the beach. I took one look at little Paulie as I called you, and my heart melted on the spot."

"You called me Paulie?" He laughed.

For a moment her gaze met Raoul's. "I did. You had the most gorgeous brown hair and eyes for a one-year-old. Such smooth olive skin. Chantelle kept you dressed in the cutest little white sunsuits, and you were such a good boy, always smiling. There wasn't a child around to compare to you. Of course, that's because your parents are beautiful people inside and out.

"I thought Guy was more handsome than that French movie star Louis Jourdan and your mom was even more stunning than Audrey Hepburn. When you all had to leave for Hawaii, I cried my eyes out."

Paul smiled up at her. "You did?"

"Yes. For ten days I'd had the time of my life. Your parents begged me to go with all of you. You know how generous your dad is. He said he'd pay for everything, and your mom insisted you wouldn't be happy without me. They made me feel wonderful, but I couldn't go. It was time for my classes to start."

"I wish I could remember."

She patted his shoulder. "That's why pictures

are so important. Do you know when we went to Disneyland, I pretended you were my little boy? Of course with my coloring no one would believe it, but I always said that when I grew up, I would want a little Paulie of my own. No one else would do." Her gaze met Raoul's as her words sank in.

Raoul wondered why she hadn't had children with her husband and sensed that there was more to her marriage to Theodore Stillman than she was letting on.

"Don't tell Giles you used to call me Paulie. He'll tell everybody."

She kissed his cheek. "Don't worry. It'll be our secret."

Paul looked at Raoul. "Promise you won't tell, either?"

He had to clear the lump in his throat before he could talk. "I swear."

"Good." He reached for his Ipod and began listening to his music while he played with his game.

Raoul ate his breakfast and looked through

the album, always coming back to the page that revealed a history he'd known nothing about. Laura waited until he'd finished his last roll, then she took his tray to the house. When she returned, he was waiting for her.

"Why didn't you tell me?" he ground out.

Her delicately arched brows met in a frown. "I assumed you knew. Don't you remember the time they went on that long trip?"

"Yes, but I never connected their activities with you."

"I guess it didn't occur to them to remind you of it. Even so, what difference does it make?"

He shot out of the chair. "You know damn well it makes every difference. I thought you were a total stranger!"

"It's been eleven years. For all intents and purposes, I *am*. You have every right to want to protect your loved ones, Raoul. Did you tell Chantelle and Guy you had suspicions about me?"

"No." Raoul had kept his feelings to himself

and allowed them to blind his opinions toward Laura.

"That's too bad. You could have saved yourself some initial grief."

"Laura," His voice grated. He'd said unconscionable things to her. "I already told Paul I was taking the two of you out on the boat with me today. Giles can come, too, if he wants." He took a deep breath. "I'd like us to start over again."

Out of wooden lips she said, "You mean no pistols at dawn?"

"None. No swords, slings or arrows. I'll come unarmed."

One brow lifted. "Raoul Laroche, unarmed?"

He lifted his hands.

A faint smile curved one corner of her pliant mouth. "You look about as innocent as Vercingetorix before he swept down on Gergovia, but it might be worth my trouble."

Raoul burst into laughter. "I had no idea you were so knowledgeable about Gallic history."

"Chantelle is a fan of one of the most famous French warriors in history."

His heart rate sped up. "If you have any other conditions, I'll do my utmost to grant them."

Their gazes fused. "For one day I'd like you to show up without your glasses."

"I don't wear any. My eyesight is 20/20."

"I'm talking about those lenses you look through from the inside. You might like what you see without them."

If he liked what he saw any more than what was in front of him right now, he was in danger of being consumed by her fire.

A few hours later Laura came up from the galley of the cruiser with two orange drinks for the boys. She arranged the large umbrella so Paul stayed out of the hot, late-afternoon sun.

"Will you two be all right if Raoul and I take a swim? We'll stay near the boat of course." She made sure his sore leg was elevated.

Paul nodded. Both of them were too involved in their electronic games to talk.

"Then we'll see you in a little while."

"Ciao," they both said at the same time.

She walked to the rear of the big cruiser where Raoul was waiting by the ladder. In black trunks his powerful, tanned body took her breath. Laura felt his black eyes roam over her as she removed her beach coat.

He'd been the perfect host so far, but this would be the first time they had been alone since taking the boat out.

"I swear the Italians invented the greatest word in the world."

"You mean *ciao,*" he surmised correctly.

Laura nodded. "You can have a whole conversation with it. Hi—goodbye—and in English it sounds like 'chow,' meaning food."

He chuckled. "Lunch was delicious by the way."

"You liked my hamburgers and chips? You weren't faking it?"

His expression remained benign. "Would I do that?"

She started to say yes, then remembered their pact. "I'm glad, then."

Recognizing she'd practiced self-control, his eyes smiled, filling her with warmth. "Are you ready for our swim?"

They were anchored a couple of miles off the point of Cap Ferrat in a calm, pale-blue sea. Conditions were ideal.

"I've wanted to do this since the day I arrived." So saying she climbed up on the side and dived straight in.

"How is it?" he asked as her head bobbed up.

She treaded water. "Fantastic. It has to be close to eighty out here, a good twelve to fifteen degrees higher than the ocean off Manhattan Beach. Come on in."

He dived off the top of the ladder, reaching her in a few swift kicks. She loved the way he looked when his black hair was plastered to his head, almost as though the water brought out the primitive in him.

Pretending he was after her, she did the back stroke around the cruiser so she could watch him. Maybe he could read her mind because he stayed a body's length away while he did the front crawl, as if he were toying with her before he seized his prey. Each time his head lifted above the water, their gazes connected, making it a little more difficult for her to breathe.

She swam full circle. When she was almost to the ladder, Raoul galvanized into action. He snaked an arm around her waist and towed her with him the short distance to the bottom rung. By now her heart was fluttering like a humming-bird's.

Their mouths gravitated to each other in a long, drawn-out, saltwater kiss that shook her to the foundations. He'd locked his legs around hers, making escape impossible, but she didn't want to escape—far from it. Being with him like this had transformed her. She felt alive and treasured for herself. Odd how she'd never felt beautiful before.

His breathing sounded shallow once he'd allowed her up for air. "Let's go below deck," he murmured in a thick toned voice against her nape. "I can't begin to do what I want with you out here."

She clung to him. "We can't anyway. There's a pair of chaperones on board."

"Let's take them home. I'm going to fix you dinner at my villa where no one will be around to disturb us."

Laura kissed his jaw. "I understand you have a pool."

"I do. It's shaped like a full moon."

"Do you ever swim in it?"

"Not for years."

"Why?"

"Have you ever noticed how lonely a pool can feel when you're the only one in it?"

She rubbed her cheek against his. "Yes. Did you live there with your wife?"

"No. Danielle's from Vence. When we married, she wanted to continue living there. It's only twenty minutes from my work, so we bought a home there."

"I remember it. You drove us through the

main street after we left Tourettes. It's a charming town."

"I agree. Her parents still live there."

It was heaven to be able to talk to him like this. "How long were you married?"

His eyes played over her features. "Five years."

More than double the length of Laura's fiasco of a marriage. "Does she still live there?"

"Yes."

"Do you ever—" She looked away. "I mean, do yo—"

"No." He read her mind. "My feelings for her died long ago. Naturally I have memories of us falling in love, but not the emotions that once accompanied them."

Laura nodded. "I know what you mean."

"Then why are we wasting our time talking about the past?"

Laura didn't want to think about it, either. "Can we swim in your pool tonight?" she asked in an aching voice.

He pressed an urgent kiss to her mouth. "I'm

living for a moon bath, as long as you take it with me."

As a shiver of delight ran through her body, she heard a familiar voice call out. "Uncle Raoul? When are you coming back?"

That slight tinge of anxiety was the only power that could have wrenched her from his embrace.

CHAPTER SEVEN

BEFORE Raoul pulled into the boat slip, he saw Guy waving to him from outside the limo. Surprised to have a welcoming committee, he shut off the motor and reached for the ropes to secure the cruiser.

His brother came onboard to help Paul back to shore using his crutches. "Did you have a good time?"

The boys nodded. "We had hamburgers for lunch!"

Guy winked at Laura. "I'm partial to those myself. Come on. Your *maman* is missing you."

Laura followed them to the car with an armload of items. Raoul started to catch up with her to help, but Guy held him back.

"You have a visitor waiting for you outside your villa."

It could only be one person. "Danielle."

He nodded. "She influenced the guard to let her through the gate. She called me and said she planned to wait for you no matter how long it took."

A full-blown bash to the gut would have been more welcome. Once again Danielle's timing was unbelievable, particularly in view of his conversation with Laura earlier.

"It's all right. I'll take care of it." She'd wanted a showdown for a long time. He'd give her one, but not in his house. Their confrontation would be short and sweet, then he'd go for Laura and take her back home with him.

"One more thing," Guy said. "Have you made a decision on the warehouse at the marina?"

"I have, and I don't think it's worth it."

"Have you told Jean-Luc yet?"

"No."

"Then do it tonight. While you're at it, tell him

you want all gossip stopped and stamped out immediately about the woman he saw you kissing last week or we're taking him off the payroll."

"You're referring to Laura of course."

"You know I am." Guy sounded angry. Possibly angrier than Raoul had ever heard him before.

"I'll do it right now if you wish. May I ask why?"

"No. My reasons are personal."

The heat of anger flared up in him. "What exactly did she tell you?"

"It's what Jean-Luc told me! Why else would Danielle show up on the estate and force her way in? She's out to cause trouble, and I won't have Laura dragged into the mess. She saved my life, *mon frère.* Do you have any comprehension of what that means to me?" His voice literally shook.

If Raoul didn't know before, he did now. He couldn't remember the last time Guy had pulled the older-brother routine on him.

"Laura has influenced Chantelle to do things

I wouldn't have imagined. I don't know what we'd do without her and I don't want to find out. I trust you to deal with the situation, Raoul."

After he walked back to the limo and it disappeared around the incline, Raoul got Jean-Luc on the line. It was too late for damage control, but an edict from Guy would ensure the agent's cooperation from here on out.

With that taken care of, he called Danielle on his cell phone. The second she picked up he said, "I'm down at the dock. If you want to talk, it will have to be here. Otherwise you'll be waiting there indefinitely."

"I just want to know one thing. Are you involved with that American woman living with Guy and Chantelle?"

Jean-Luc hadn't wasted any time. Raoul had no one but himself to blame and instantly regretted his impulsive actions from that day. Guy was right, it wasn't fair to drag Laura into this mess. "We've been divorced a year, Danielle. My business is my own."

"You *are* involved!" she cried emotionally. "How much does she mean to you, Raoul?"

That was a question Raoul didn't even want to think about, because he knew that the answer would disturb him. "I'm hanging up now, Danielle."

"You can't marry her, Raoul! You can't, I won't let you!"

He clicked off, then phoned security and told them to escort his ex-wife off the estate. Danielle needed help, and he'd begged her to get it when they were married, had offered to pay for it, but she had always refused.

Ironically, though, she'd just hit on the truth. Laura was still Ted Stillman's wife and out of bounds. But Raoul was determined to find out why she was still married to the man, because he knew she couldn't be in love with him anymore.

After he reached his villa he received another call, this time from the deputy minister of finance in Paris. The other man was calling an emergency meeting of the economic committee first thing in the morning. Raoul needed to bring all the latest banking figures with him.

He groaned. To get all that together would take him till midnight. This was one meeting he couldn't get out of. The night he'd anticipated with Laura would have to be put off. He was beginning to believe the last few hours had been nothing more than an unattainable dream.

When he tried to reach her to explain, Guy said she was in with Paul. Totally frustrated, he told his brother he had to fly to Paris and would get in touch with Laura later. Guy said he'd tell her, but he sounded more preoccupied than usual. After they hung up, he headed for his bedroom and started throwing things in his suitcase.

The maid knocked on Laura's door the next morning and brought her a breakfast tray. On her way out she asked Laura if she needed anything washed. She did actually. It forced her to get up and face the day. After the heavenly afternoon she'd spent with Raoul, her disappointment over not being with him last night had just about killed her.

Once dressed in shorts and a T-shirt, she put her hair in a ponytail and went in search of Chantelle, who would have had breakfast by now. Another maid informed her Guy had left to take Paul to Remy's house, but he'd be back shortly. In an aside she mentioned that Chantelle was having a bad morning. When Laura asked if she was ill, the maid shook her head. Guy's wife had been crying and wouldn't stop.

There could be many reasons for her tears. Laura vacillated between doing a little gardening or going to check on her. In the end she walked down the other hall to the master suite. The minute she put her ear to the door, she heard heartwrenching sobs coming out of Chantelle, the kind that couldn't be dismissed.

Deciding to take the chance she might get told to leave the villa and never come back, Laura opened the door and tiptoed inside. Beyond their sitting room was the master bedroom, but her sobs came from an adjoining room. Evidently she and Guy lived in separate rooms.

The door to Chantelle's room stood ajar. Laura looked in. Chantelle sat on an upholstered bench in front of her dressing table with her head buried in her hands. The wheelchair was pushed away. She wore a lovely lemon-colored nightgown. It looked like she'd been brushing her dark chestnut hair. Such a beautiful woman. No wonder Guy was beside himself.

Taking a deep breath she said, "Chantelle?"

She lifted her head to reveal a glistening wet face. "Please leave me alone."

Laura was prepared for that. "I can't. It's because I see myself in you. No one sobs the way you're doing unless you've reached the breaking point. I reached mine six months ago. If my best friend hadn't intervened and helped me to leave Ted, I don't know what I would have done.

"I didn't come in here for Guy's sake. He's gone with Paul. I came for me because I can't bear to see you in this kind of pain." She moved closer and hunkered down next to her. Looking into her eyes she said, "You've got to talk to someone. Let me be a sounding board. Please."

In the quiet, a gold and crystal clock with angels moving their parts chimed ten o'clock. Laura waited, holding her breath.

"I'm dying, Laura," Chantelle said in a dull voice. "I have a brain tumour and I am going to die."

She didn't say it hysterically. It came out as a statement of fact.

Laura fought her own hysteria.

"When did you find out?"

"Right after the accident when they did a CAT scan and an MRI. They found it and said it was inoperable. If I hadn't had the car accident, I wouldn't have known until the symptoms began to appear. They said I would start to show signs within three to four months and be dead within a year."

"Obviously, Guy doesn't know anything about this."

"No. He'll find out soon enough."

"That's why you've been pushing him away?"

"Yes. I know my husband. We love and need each other too much. I decided to distance myself so that when things get difficult, it won't be such a shock to him. He and Paul have each other."

Laura groaned inwardly at Chantelle's desperate situation. "Have the symptoms started?"

"Two migraines."

What Chantelle was doing was more painful for Guy than the death sentence, but in Chantelle's mind she'd chosen to handle it this way. Laura wouldn't be able to talk her out of it. Without hesitation she wrapped her arms around her and rocked her for a long time.

"You can never tell him, Laura."

"No. I won't. But this is affecting everyone, Chantelle. Not just Guy but Paul, too. It's even been hard on Raoul. He loves you and has resented me for being here to try to help when he can't."

"I know. I purposely didn't tell him we knew you previously."

"Why?" Laura couldn't believe what she was hearing.

"The more he's distracted, the more he leaves me alone. He was born with extra radar. He's not like Guy. Since his divorce and my accident, he's over here constantly, always trying to get me to do things, hoping I'll turn back into the old Chantelle. I can't bear his scrutiny."

Laura could relate to that, too. "That's because he loves you so much."

"I love Raoul, too. He is a wonderful brother to me. That's what has made this so much harder."

She bit her lip. "How can I help you, Chantelle?"

"I want you to stay with us to the end. Paul would be thrilled, and he'll need you when the time comes. Would it be possible, Laura?"

"I…I don't know." There was too much to process at once.

Chantelle stared at her through drenched eyes. "When Guy said you were calling from Italy, I couldn't have been happier and told him to invite you to the house. It's like my prayers had been answered. Little did I know you would save his life that night! I love you, Laura, my family loves you. We need you now."

Laura took a fortifying breath. "I'm going to have to speak to my boss again."

"You'll be safe with us. I'd like to see that husband of yours try to bother you here. Guy wouldn't stand for it."

Right now Laura's thoughts weren't on Ted. She was envisioning everyone's pain and trauma over the next few months when Chantelle started degenerating. The thought of it was unbearable.

"Guy's going to be back soon. Let's go out to the rose garden so he won't know you've been crying."

"I'll get dressed."

They hugged for another long moment before Laura left the room.

She wished she could wave a magic wand and restore Chantelle to the happiness of her life before the accident. To think she'd been living all these months knowing she had an inoperable brain tumor…

For herself, Laura wished she could run into one pair of arms for comfort and know she would always be welcome there. While Raoul was still in Paris, the only panacea for her pain was work, whether it be helping with Paul, doing some gardening or keeping Chantelle company.

By the next evening she was ready to make that important phone call to her boss. While she was at it, she wanted to send him her latest artwork. In order to do it, she needed access to a scanner.

Laura glanced at Paul, who'd used his crutches to walk her over to Raoul's villa from Guy's. His leg was healing so well he really didn't need crutches anymore. She couldn't get over how agile he was again.

"Are you sure your uncle won't mind?"

"Nope. I use his stuff whenever I need it for school. *Maman* gave you her permission. He won't be home until tomorrow night. She said that conference in Paris ran over another day. Come on in."

Raoul's home was more contemporarily furnished, but equally elegant. "This is a beautiful place."

"My grandparents used to live here, but I don't remember them. Papa said they died in a plane accident." She'd wondered about Raoul's parents, yet another scar to add to his damaged heart. "Sit over here and I'll show you how his scanner works."

Laura had brought all three sketchpads she'd filled so far this trip. She needed to download everything she scanned and e-mail it. Depending on what her boss thought of her work, she'd broach the subject of staying in France for an indefinite period. As much as she wanted a divorce from Ted, Chantelle had become her top priority.

It would mean taking a leave of absence from her lifeguard job. Plus she'd have to discuss the whole situation of her apartment with Cindy.

After a few run-throughs with Paul on Raoul's state-of-the-art equipment, she felt she could take it from here. "You're a whiz, *mon ami.*" He'd been teaching her some basic phrases. "I think I'm ready, thanks to you. Why don't you go now. Giles is waiting for you."

"Call the house if you have problems."

"I don't plan to have any."

He grinned. *"Ciao."*

"Ciao."

Once she got the knack of it, the scanning went fast. Before long she'd done the downloading. A press of the button and they were sent. Before she left to go back to the other villa she phoned her boss. He'd be in his office by now. It was after 9:00 a.m. his time.

"Other World Video Games."

'Hi, Sandra. It's Laura. Can I speak to Carl?"

"Sure. Just a moment."

While she waited, she studied a grouping of small-framed pictures on the shelf above his desk. She reached for one of them. Raoul and

Guy were just young boys surrounded by family. Laura loved them so much she wanted to steal them.

"Laura? How are you?"

"I'm fine, Carl. And you?"

"Swamped as usual. What's going on?"

"I wanted you to know I just sent you a file of all my sketches."

"Terrific! Let me take a look while you're on the line."

While they were busy chatting about business, she heard an ear-piercing whistle. "These are fabulous, Laura! I mean really fabulous!"

"Oh, good. I'm glad you like them."

"Like—the guys in the backroom are going to go crazy! Don't you ever leave me, honey."

Carl was the only man she didn't mind calling her that. "Actually, that's what I'm calling about."

"No. I'm not going to listen."

She laughed. "I have to be serious for a moment." In the next breath she explained her dilemma and ended up in tears.

When she'd finished he said, "Let me sleep on it and we'll talk tomorrow at the same time."

"Thanks, Carl."

"Thank *you.* By the way, Sandra's been documenting the number of calls your husband has made to the office. She has the telephone company printouts. The pile is growing."

"It's *his* funeral, but I'm sorry you've been bothered. Tell her I owe her."

"No problem. Talk to you tomorrow."

"Tomorrow." She clicked off.

"What's so important about tomorrow?"

Laura spun around in the swivel chair. "Raoul—"

He wasn't supposed to be home until tomorrow night. She shivered to think that if he'd come in a few minutes sooner, he would have heard her telling Carl about Chantelle's condition. The little picture she was holding fell on the area rug. "Oh, I'm sorry." She rushed to pick it up and dropped her cell phone.

Raoul was there so fast their hands brushed.

He was still in his gray business suit. When he lifted his dark head, their faces were level. Mere centimeters apart. It only took a little tug to pull her down on the floor next to him.

"On the flight home I wondered how I was going to get you alone before the evening was out."

She'd made up her mind they couldn't do this until she was free from Ted, but her puny efforts to resist were no match for his hard-muscled strength. He stretched out on his back and pulled her on top of him. Taking his time he threaded his fingers through the fine-spun gold of her hair.

"Umm…you've been out in the sun this afternoon." He kissed every feature of her face. "Much as I like the taste of your lipstick, I like the taste of the strawberries you had for dinner. They're sweet like your mouth. You'd have to be a man to know what it does to me."

With one hand at the back of her waist, the other spanning her neck, he gathered her tightly against him, searching for her mouth until they clung in a wine-dark rapture.

One kiss. That was all. It started out slow, then began building, shooting fire through her body until she felt an ecstasy almost beyond bearing. Somewhere outside the euphoric haze holding her in its thrall she heard the phone ringing.

"Raoul—" she moaned helplessly, but he wasn't listening. In a dizzying motion she was turned on her back, her face cupped between his hands. He lowered his mouth to her eyelids and earlobes.

"You're gorgeous," he whispered in an aching voice. "I can't get enough. Three days away from you have been an eternity." His lips swept over her cheeks and throat before coming back to her mouth over and over again in a rhythm so intoxicating, he might as well be putting her under a spell.

He was the vortex drawing her in with a hold so strong she had no concept of time or knew where she was.

"Laura?" She heard Paul on the voice message. "*Maman* said to call and tell you Uncle Raoul is home so you won't be surprised."

"I should call him back," she said, trying to roll away from him.

"He doesn't expect a response."

Raoul slid his hands to her shoulders from behind. The second he touched her, she felt like she was undergoing a meltdown. He removed the picture she was holding in her hand. "I like this one, too," he murmured into her hair. "I'm eight here. Guy's fourteen. Give me some time and I'll show you *my* baby pictures."

She'd love to see them, but her heartache over Chantelle was too great to get back to the happiness she'd experienced a few days ago out on the cruiser. Slowly she moved away from him and started gathering up her sketches.

He put the picture back on the shelf while his gaze remained riveted on her. "What's wrong? Where have you gone since I left?"

She could try to keep her heart from hammering, but when she was anywhere near Raoul, her body reacted with a will that knew no master. This time, however, it was vital she deflect his radar, a precarious assignment under any circumstances, but especially now.

"While you've been in Paris, there's been a development."

Over the past seventy-two hours she'd been forced to come to grips with the knowledge that Chantelle's days were numbered. There'd been more nights when Laura had cried herself to sleep because she'd had to bear the burden of it alone. Now there were two inconsolable women in the villa.

His body tensed. She could see it in the rigidity of his jaw. "Go on."

"Chantelle has asked me to stay on longer than the two weeks."

Raoul shrugged out of his suit jacket and tossed it over a chair back. Rolling up his shirtsleeves he said, "I don't understand why that's so upsetting to you when it's clear the family adores you. Did you say yes?"

She rubbed her temples. "Not yet."

Through slumberous eyes he examined her face and figure. "Come into the kitchen with me and you can tell me why. The heat in Paris was stifling. I need something cold to drink."

Whether she should or not, she followed him through his beautiful home to the immaculate kitchen. He opened the fridge and pulled out a bottled water. "Would you like one, too? I don't have anything else to offer. I haven't entertained since my divorce. I'm afraid my cupboards are embarrassingly empty."

"Please." After removing the lid, he put the cold bottle against her hot cheek for a minute. She could almost hear it sizzle before he placed it in her hand. She took a long gulp while he began drinking his. At one point their gazes collided. Her hand tightened on the bottleneck in reaction to that penetrating look. "If you came to my apartment in Manhattan Beach, I couldn't even offer you water."

He drained the rest and put the empty bottle

on the counter. "Does that mean you're inviting me?" The depth of his tone traveled to her insides, causing her to grow weak with the longing to experience more of his passion. He was like a drug her system recognized and wanted above everything else.

"I wish I could," her voice shook.

Shadows marred his handsome features. "What's the hold your husband has on you?"

It was time for the truth. "I fell out of love with Ted soon after we were married. I'm trying to divorce him, but he's giving me trouble."

There was a moment of quiet before he said, "How long were you married before you filed?"

She took a fortifying breath. "Two years."

"How did you meet him?"

"He was out on the family yacht with a group of friends. They'd come down the coast from Santa Barbara. It was a beautiful day, but there was some wind that had kicked up moderate swells. Four of them decided to swim in the ocean for a little while. I was on lifeguard duty.

"I'm always looking through my binoculars for signs of trouble. You can usually tell when a person is starting to drown because their hands go up and their head goes back. While I was spotting different people, I saw this swimmer struggling and raced out."

"Ted, obviously."

She nodded. "When I brought him in to shore, he was in serious trouble. It took a long time to revive him. The paramedics arrived and took over, but they didn't give him much of a chance to survive. A week later I had a phone call from my supervisor telling me that Congressman Stillman wanted to meet me."

"I think I can write the script from here."

"It's transparent." She laughed sadly. "One thing led to another and I met the older man and his son, Ted. They wanted to thank me for saving Ted's life. In fact they were so grateful they couldn't do enough for me. Flowers, dinner at their home."

Raoul's brow lowered. "Sounds like Guy and Chantelle."

"But there's one huge difference," she declared. "Guy hoped I might be able to help Chantelle. Ted pursued me relentlessly. I was attracted and fell hard for him. He decided he would marry me. I became his trophy wife."

The use of that word made his lips thin.

"He never shared his dream with me about going into politics. I was a naive fool to think we could have a normal life. He insisted I be in all his photo shoots."

"I saw one of you on the Colorado River."

She bowed her head. "That was a nightmare trip. They all were. We were never home to make a home. Ted demanded I give up both my jobs and be available to him for his campaign. He liked the idea of being a young, hip congressman with a wife he could show off.

"Too late I realized he had no depth and was just using me. In fact Ted could only love himself. I saved his life and he mistook it for love. So did I. His father encouraged our union because to quote him, 'I looked good in print.'"

"You can't blame him for that," he said under his breath, but she heard him.

"Toward the end of our marriage, I refused to go on any more trips with him. His mother begged me to work things out with him one more time. So I showed up at his hotel one night and discovered him with another woman."

Raoul bit out an epithet.

"One of his ex-security men told me it was the usual pattern with the Stillman men. I went back home. On the advice of my friend, Cindy, I found an attorney who wouldn't be intimidated by the Stillmans and I filed for divorce."

"When was that?"

"Six months ago. Ted's been fighting it ever since. He's afraid a divorce will finish him in politics. The Stillman family has never had a divorce. Their record is clean, so to speak, so he has refused to give me one.

"When I return to Manhattan Beach I'll take him to court. With the documentation I've accrued, the judge will have to grant it unless he's in their pocket, but I have to be careful."

He squinted at her. “Why?”

“As I told Guy, Ted’s been having me followed in the hope than he can get something on me to hold up the divorce. My attorney told me to stay out of the limelight. I’m still a married woman so I have to be careful not to give him an opportunity to get a photo of me with a man that could be misconstrued in any way.”

He gave her a brooding stare “You mean like a picture of me kissing you down by the marina that day.”

She nodded.

“I’m sorry,” his voice grated.

“It doesn’t matter. I’m just glad Jean-Luc wasn’t working for Ted. I don’t want anything to hold up my divorce, but now that Chantelle has asked me stay longer, it puts a court date off that much further.” She stared at him. “Did your wife fight your divorce?”

His chest rose and fell sharply. “Yes, but I had the resources to end it quickly. Is lack of money the only problem holding you up?”

She nodded. "I earn enough from both jobs to pay my attorney in increments. He's willing to carry the loan for as many years as it takes me. My problem is, if I stay here, I can't work so I can't build up my savings."

"You know Guy would give you any amount you need."

"I believe he would, but I'd never take it. The Stillmans use their money to buy people and favors. Being married to Ted sickened me on the subject."

"Certain marriages have a way of doing that," he muttered.

It was time to get off the subject that had brought deep pain to both of them.

"Raoul…Chantelle said I could use your scanner, but I still want to thank you. I decided to send my latest sketches to my boss. It was a good time to ask him if he thought he could give me a leave of absence so I'll have a job to return to after Chantelle…no longer needs me."

He moved closer. "So you've decided you'll stay?"

"Yes. In fact, I'd like to get back to the villa and tell her before she goes to bed."

"Then don't let me stop you."

Somehow she hadn't expected he would allow things to end this way. She'd thought he would pull her into his arms and beg her not to go, but obviously he was still battling some dark places in his psyche, left over from his divorce.

CHAPTER EIGHT

WITH her phone in hand, Laura paced the floor of her bedroom. “You’re sure you don’t mind, Cindy?”

“What else do I have to do? Bringing in the mail and letting the cleaning crew in once a week is nothing! I haven’t seen your husband since last time. Is that good or bad?”

“I don’t know, but I can’t thank you enough. I’ll make it up to you.”

“You already have by letting me drive your car when I need one.”

“It has to be driven once in a while.”

“Agreed. Now tell me about Raoul.”

“I haven’t seen him for close to a week. He left for Switzerland again, and now I’ve learned he’s been in Lyon.”

"I bet you're dying."

"I am." Laura didn't know if these trips were partially because he was in some kind of pain he still couldn't bring himself to share with her.

"How long a sabbatical has Carl given you?" Cindy asked, tactfully changing the subject.

"We worked out two and a half more months. More than that and he'll have to hire someone else."

"But Chantelle might live another year. No one ever really knows about these things."

"I know. I'd give anything to talk to her doctor, but of course I can't."

"What about Raoul, do you think you can tell him?"

"I don't know, Cindy. They are such a close family, it is surely going to destroy them. I don't know how I am going to go on keeping this secret to myself for much longer, but I don't want to break Chantelle's trust in me."

Cindy paused before answering. "I think you know Raoul better than most people, and it seems to me that he is the one you should trust with this. Think about it, Laura, it might help them more than they know right now."

"You're right, Cindy, I'll think about what you said. Anyway, enough of that. I won't keep you any longer. Call me anytime."

Laura hung up the phone feeling guilty their conversations always kept Cindy up past midnight. But her friend insisted it was the best time. Thank heaven for her; she provided a much-needed outlet. They both did for each other.

She moved off the bed and went into the bathroom to brush her hair. By now Chantelle would be ready for a morning swim. Laura changed out of her nightgown to her swimsuit and left the bedroom for the patio.

Normally Chantelle was already sitting there eating toast and drinking her coffee. Laura sat down to breakfast without her. She'd be along, but when it got to be 10:00 a.m. and there was still no sign of her, Laura began to get nervous. Maybe she was having one of her crying spells.

After checking with the maid, who hadn't

seen her, Laura decided to go to her bedroom as she'd done once before. This time when she walked in, she found Chantelle in her swimsuit and beach robe, but she was lying across the bed, white-faced.

Alarmed, Laura leaned over her. "Chantelle? Are you having another migraine?"

"Yes. I've taken my prescription for it. Give me another half hour and it will pass."

A cold hand squeezed her heart. This was the second attack since Laura had been in Cap Ferrat. "Can I get you an ice pack?"

"It doesn't help. All I need is quiet and no light."

"Then I'll go." Laura felt horrible she'd disturbed her.

Guy phoned. He always did this time of day to see if his wife needed anything. When Laura picked up and told him about her headache, he said he was coming home from the office. The poor thing couldn't get any work done while Chantelle was like this.

By the time he arrived, Laura had showered

and dressed for the day in a plum colored skirt with a matching print top. She'd arranged her hair in a French twist at the back of her head secured with a tortoiseshell comb.

Since Guy had come home, she told him she would ask Pierre to drive her into Nice to pick up some of Chantelle's favorite chocolate truffles. His wife loved one in the afternoon with a cup of coffee.

Guy told her to take as long as she wanted. He wasn't going anywhere. Raoul had returned from Switzerland and would be handling everything at the office until further notice.

Her pulse raced just hearing that unexpected news. Without wasting any time, she left the villa. Pierre knew exactly where to go in Nice. Within a half hour she'd made her purchase, but when he asked her if she was ready to return to the villa, she said no. In the next breath she told him to drive her to Laroche headquarters and asked if he would wait for her.

After Pierre pulled up in front, she climbed out

and rushed inside the luxurious office building located outside the old part of the city. The security guard near the elevators told her she wouldn't be able to see Monsieur Laroche without an appointment.

"Please ring and tell him it's Mrs. Aldridge on an urgent matter."

He did her bidding, then told her to wait. After he'd made the call, his attitude changed. Suddenly he apologized all over the place, offering her his seat and a drink if she'd like one. She shook her head.

Whatever Raoul had said had lit a fire under him. It had the effect of a soothing balm because she hadn't known what kind of reception she would get. Raoul ran hot and cold depending on his mood and the situation at the moment. Evidently, he didn't want her going up to his office suite, so she had no choice but to wait.

"Laura?" sounded that deep husky voice she'd missed so horribly. She whirled around to discover Raoul striding up to her dressed in a midnight-blue suit and dazzling white shirt with a monogrammed tie. He was too attractive. She could hardly breathe.

He'd come down a private elevator further along the hall. She could tell because there weren't any buttons. You had to use a specially coded card key made for a select few.

His eyes played everywhere, setting her on fire. She could hear it crackling, could feel the tremendous rise in temperature heating her body.

"I…I hope you don't mind me bothering you here at work, especially when Guy said you just flew in, but this is vital."

Something in her demeanor must have told him she wasn't kidding because his expression grew solemn. "How did you get here?"

"With Pierre. He's out in front."

She heard his sharp intake of breath. "Let's go."

He didn't touch her, but she sensed he wanted to. Whatever black mood he'd been in a week ago seemed to have dissipated. With the sparks they were setting off right now, the slightest provocation made them combustible.

She noticed he sat opposite her once they were enclosed inside the limo, as if he didn't trust himself to be next to her. It was just as well since she didn't trust herself. He signaled to Pierre to take them home, but she shook her head.

"I have to talk to you first. Ask him to wait."

"What's this all about? I thought you made a commitment to Chantelle to stay."

Where had that come from? A fierce look had taken hold of his features. Could she hope that she'd grown on him enough that he couldn't tolerate the idea of her leaving?

She wasn't talking about their physical chemistry, which was so powerful she quaked with yearning if she allowed herself to remember that night at his villa. She was thinking of emotions that drove two people together and kept them that way for a lifetime because they didn't need anyone else to complete them.

Guy and Chantelle were the perfect example of what she was talking about. On a moment's notice he'd left work to be at her side, even if she pretended she didn't want him there, because he loved her. It was because of that love Laura couldn't live with her secret any longer.

She'd promised Chantelle she wouldn't tell anyone, but she had wrestled with her conscience long enough and had to break her silence, for everyone's sake.

"This isn't about me. Chantelle's home with a migraine."

A bleakness entered his eyes. "I know. Guy said he was going home to be there for her. She gets them on occasion."

Laura had never prayed harder in her life that she was doing the right thing. "I know why she gets them, Raoul. I know everything."

A stillness invaded the car's interior. A grim expression crossed over his striking features. "You know the reason for her behavior since the accident?" he whispered in shock.

Laura nodded. "Last week I found her sobbing. She lay across her bed like a forlorn little doll, white as her sheets. She told me to leave, but I insisted on staying until she admitted what was going on. That's when it all came out.

"After she was taken to the hospital following her car accident, she found out she had an inoperable brain tumor and was given less than a year to live."

"What?" Raoul looked as if he'd just heard that life as they knew it was about to be obliterated.

She swallowed hard. "It's taken me time to comprehend what she told me, so I can only imagine what you're feeling right now. It isn't fair what's happened to her, but then life really isn't fair." Her voice shook.

"Start from the beginning," he demanded through lips that looked as chiseled as the rest of his features.

"Though she didn't tell me, she must have sworn the doctors to secrecy. After being utterly devastated by the news, she came up with the idea to push Guy—all of you—away, in order to prepare you for her death.

"Her migraines are purely stress related because of the secret she's been holding back." For the next few minutes Laura told him everything she knew and remembered of their conversation.

When she'd finished, Raoul's mouth had gone white around the edges. His black eyes impaled her. "It's been a whole week. You should have come to me the moment you knew."

"She swore me to secrecy, Raoul, and she trusts me. If you only knew how I've been struggling ever since. You know how deeply I care for her. I couldn't stand it if I lost the trust she has in me. But in the end I couldn't keep it in. That's why I finally came to you."

"To lie to this degree…" He bit out and shook his dark head. "Chantelle couldn't possibly love Guy the way I thought she did—the way *he* thought she did.

"For over three months she's caused excruciating pain to her own husband, to her son. To me," he said scathingly. "This news will destroy my brother. What kind of woman does that to a man?"

"Don't," Laura begged him. "You couldn't begin to know what frame of mind she was in after the accident. She was still in shock when they told her." Laura leaned across to put a hand on his forearm It was hard as steel. There was no give, even with her entreating him.

"Raoul," she said softly. Seeing him in so much pain was devastating.

He ignored her entreaty and pulled out his phone. After he told the driver to take them home, he lay back against the seat with his eyes closed, his pallor unmistakable. They didn't talk the rest of the way.

The minute Pierre stopped the limo, Raoul hurried inside the villa with her. Laura didn't know how he was going to broach the subject to his brother, but she was terrified.

Her heart sank when one of the maids saw them in the foyer and came over to Raoul. She explained that Guy had taken Madame to the hospital because the pain had gotten worse. Paul was at Giles's house.

"You go," Laura cried as he turned to her. "She needs her family." What if the end was coming sooner than the doctor thought? "If Paul should phone, I'll tell him."

He nodded grim-faced and rushed out of the villa.

"Guy?" Raoul whispered. "While Chantelle's still asleep, we need to talk. Come out in the hall with me."

He shook his head. "I don't want to leave her."

Since the conversation in the limo with Laura, Raoul was alive with grief and rage. The morphine cocktail drip helping Chantelle to recover from this latest migraine brought home the reality of her true condition. Seeing her stretched out on the examining table, helpless, was killing him.

In the two hours he'd been at the hospital with his brother, the color had returned to her cheeks.

Both he and Guy breathed easier because of it, but Raoul didn't want to wait any longer to tell him the brutal truth.

With reluctance Guy got up from the chair and followed Raoul to the reception area outside the E.R. where half a dozen people were sitting around waiting. Raoul purposely walked him down a corridor. When he found an empty examining room, he pulled him inside and shut the door.

"Sit down, Guy. I have something to tell you."

"I can't sit."

He eyed his brother soulfully. "You're going to need to."

Guy's face went ashen before he did Raoul's bidding.

"I know the reason for the drastic change in Chantelle."

His eyes widened. "She told Laura?" Lines of exhaustion from worry made him seem older.

This was the hardest thing Raoul had ever had to do in his life. "Yes. I just came from talking to her. There's no easy way to say this, so I'm just going to go ahead. Chantelle is dying of an inoperable brain tumor."

By now Raoul would have told Guy the heartbreaking news. Since Laura couldn't do anything for anyone, she decided to fly to Marseille and take a tourist boat out from the port to the Château d'If a mile away. This was one time when she needed to get away from the villa. Guy had told Laura to use the helicopter anytime she wanted. It was at her disposal.

Armed with a couple of new sketchpads and pencils, she embarked on her journey. She needed to immerse herself in work for a few hours to deal with the pain.

Dumas had made the fortress famous in his novel of *The Count of Monte Cristo,* which Laura had read years earlier. According to Chantelle, it was a square, three-story castle built by François I in the early 1500s. The perfect kind of setting for a videogame.

Her drawing ended up taking the whole afternoon. There was one more level of the castle to go before she went back to the mainland.

Despite the tourists milling around, Laura had managed to fill a sketchpad already. The guide at the château had explained that the former prisoners were treated differently depending on their wealth and social class. Edmond Dantes, the prisoner in Dumas's novel, had been incarcerated at the bottom of the dungeon below the waterline. No windows, no amenities.

Wealthier inmates, on the second level, had their own private cells. Each level was different enough to make up a unique game. The top of the castle had been built for prisoners who had outside help to pay for the privilege. There were windows, a fireplace and a garderobe. The whole château was a natural. Once a player mastered the dungeon level, he could move on up to the second level and then the third.

Deep in concentration on the last page of her drawings, she was scarcely aware of the activity going on around her. "Didn't you hear the guide?" a man said near her ear. "They're closing for the day."

The sound of his voice was so familiar to her, it caused her to drop her sketchpad. Raoul picked it up before she could and looked through it. "The same quality, the same verve," he muttered.

"Thank you." The words came out close to a whisper because she was so amazed to see him here. He'd been on her mind continually. If he'd already told Guy, she couldn't tell. In the dim light his eyes had never looked so jet-black.

"The pilot's waiting to fly us back. Let's go."

She put her sketchpad in her tote bag and followed him down the ancient stone stairs to the entrance. They took the tender back to the mainland. Within a half hour they'd landed on the estate, where the limo was waiting. Raoul told the driver to drop them off at his villa.

All the while she'd had to contain her misery while she waited to hear the worst. When he ushered her inside his living room, she couldn't stand it any longer and wheeled around. "If you don't tell me what's happened, I don't think I can stand it."

He removed his suit jacket and tie before standing in front of her. "As we speak, Guy, Chantelle and Paul are at the hospital in a private room while she's still recovering from her migraine."

The tears she'd been fighting gushed down her cheeks. "It must be so awful, I can't bear it."

"You could say Guy came close to losing it when he demanded to meet with all her doctors. Then a strange thing happened." He cocked his head. "They all denied she had a brain tumor. To prove it, they did another MRI on her. It only took ten minutes. They found nothing on her brain of any kind."

"What did you say?" Laura cried.

"When Chantelle awakened from the medication, they asked where she had got the idea she was dying. She told them exactly what she told you. So they called in the attending E.R. physician who was on call the day of her accident. It appears that while she was lying there, she overheard him talking to another doctor about another patient who'd been brought in."

"You mean Chantelle's not dying?" Her voice sound more like a shriek.

He shook his head. "She's in perfect health."

"Oh, Raoul, thank God!" She flew toward him and threw her arms around him, sobbing. She must have hugged him for ten minutes.

"Thank God," he eventually said in a gravelly voice, but something was missing. Where was his joy? She didn't understand and eased out of his arms to look at him.

What she saw in his expression alarmed her. She knew he was exhausted from his business trip. Coupled with his agony over Chantelle, he looked dissipated, though she knew he wasn't. Even in this state he was devastatingly attractive, but he was definitely behaving strangely.

Her anxiety was at a pitch. She searched for a reason. "Can't Guy forgive her?" she cried.

Raoul stood planted there as still as a piece of driftwood left high and dry on a lonely beach.

"I have absolutely no idea, but I do know this. If Chantelle were my wife, I couldn't forgive her." Suddenly his eyes pierced hers like lasers. "I'm convinced there's no such thing as an honest woman."

His words sounded the death knell to their tender relationship.

Raoul couldn't forgive Laura for keeping Chantelle's secret from everyone for a whole week. He might as well have said, "Get out of my sight and never come back."

Her body shrank from the knowledge. She turned away from him and ran out of the villa. As soon as she could pack her things, Raoul would get his wish.

CHAPTER NINE

THE judge adjusted his bifocals. This was it. Laura held her breath while her attorney squeezed her arm to give her courage. He read:

> "In the matter of *Stillman v. Stillman,* the case brought before the Court of Santa Barbara in the County of Santa Barbara, California, the Court has read the petition for divorce on the grounds of incompatibility and finds all documentation in order. Therefore a decree of divorce between Laurel Aldridge and Theodore Stillman has been granted on this fifteenth day of August.

"Counselors will get together on your own time to agree on disbursement of monies and property." He pounded his gavel. "Court adjourned." The judge stood up and left the room.

Laura swung around and hugged her attorney. "Thank you. You'll never know how I've longed for this day."

He smiled. "By keeping a low profile all these months, there was nothing your ex could find on you to try and prolong your case. Without children involved, I was able to get the earliest court date for you."

"I'm aware of all you've done for me and can never thank you enough."

"Do you know what I admire about you most, Laura? Besides refusing all money or property, you refused to charge him with adultery. One day when he's a congressman, he'll thank you for not dragging his name through the mud. His public record will remain clean. The man's luckier than he knows."

"He doesn't believe that, but whatever he thinks, it doesn't matter. It's over. Thank you again for helping me believe this day was going to come."

"It's been my pleasure. Come on. I'll walk you out."

She held on to his arm, leaving Ted and his brothers glaring at her from the other side of the aisle. She couldn't figure out why. He was free to find a new trophy wife. One who wanted it all, too.

Cindy stood waiting outside the doors of the courtroom. The minute Laura saw her she hugged her for a long time. "I'm finally free." The tears rolled down her cheeks.

"Where do you want to celebrate before I have to get back to work? Name it. It's my treat today."

Laura eased away from her and wiped her eyes. "Thanks, Cindy. How about we meet for a hamburger at the Z-Top."

"You're on, let's go."

It didn't take long to reach their rendezvous point. Once they were served, Cindy smiled at her. "Are you officially Ms. Aldridge again?"

Laura nodded. "That was part of what was

included in the decree. My whole life's going to change, not having to answer to Mrs. Stillman anymore."

"Today you're no longer a celebrity."

"Nope. Just me, thank heaven. For the last year I've envied you being free. Now I don't have to look over my shoulder every minute. I can't believe that when I go home, I don't have to worry about Ted barging in on me or phoning me at odd hours. I'm my own person, just like I used to be."

"Not quite your own person," Cindy said cryptically.

She stopped munching. "What do you mean?"

Cindy gave her that knowing look. "Raoul, of course. Ever since you flew home from Cap Ferrat you haven't been yourself. Knowing you as I do, I'd say you're emotionally drained. You've lost weight you know."

"After living at Guy's house with that cook of theirs, I needed to shed five pounds."

"Lie to anyone else, but not me. I feel responsible for having given you the wrong advice."

"But you didn't!" Laura assured her. "You posed a question I had to answer to my own satisfaction. How could you possibly be blamed for that? If I'd never phoned you, I still would have done exactly what I did. When you make a promise to someone as serious as the one I made to Chantelle, you don't break it without a darn good reason. I needed that week Raoul was gone to be certain."

"That's what makes you my best friend."

"Thanks for that, Cindy." She smoothed the hair away from her temple. "Raoul despised me for not telling him everything the second Chantelle broke down and revealed what was really going on.

"You know that old adage about the third time being the charm. Raoul's wife lied to him, couple that with the information I held back from him. Add to that Chantelle's betrayal. It was the last straw for a man whose psyche is already very dark and complicated.

"During the time I was there we'd talk for a

little bit, then he'd close up. It was inch by inch all the time. I still don't know that much about him. A man who can't communicate his deepest feelings isn't capable of having a relationship, sustained or otherwise. Raoul's one man who travels alone. That much I learned." As she spoke Laura felt a sharp pain deep in her heart at the thought of what might have been.

"I'm sorry," her friend whispered.

"So am I, but there's not a thing I can do about it. When I was at his villa, I saw these pictures of him and Guy when they were little. They both looked so happy. It's terrible to think a bad marriage can change a person that drastically.

"Once in a while I saw glimpses of another Raoul with no shadows. The only time we really communicated—" She got the pain in her chest again and couldn't go on. "You know."

"Yup. When it was good, it was very good," Cindy murmured. "That's the part I'm waiting for with Sam." Sam was Cindy's new love interest, and it had taken a while for the woman to move on after her bitter divorce, but it seemed things were finally looking up for her. Laura was delighted.

"At least you two are really talking now. Sharing. I'm envious." When it got bad with Raoul, it was the end of Laura's world. She shook her head. "I've got to stop this."

"Want to go to a film tonight? Eight o'clock-ish?"

"I was just going to suggest it. Tomorrow my lifeguarding won't start till noon so I can sleep in."

"Lucky you."

"Speaking of luck, Carl said my sketches of the Chateau d'If won me a week's vacation even though I already took extra time off in Cap Ferrat. Want to fly down to Mexico with me in September? I'm going to do some sketches of pyramids and temples while I'm there."

"Ohh. I'd love to see them. Let me talk dates with my boss and I'll get back to you."

"Good. We'll get one of those inexpensive

package that won't set us back too much." She checked her watch. "I've got to get going."

"So do I."

Laura started to put some money down, but Cindy stopped her. "I'm paying this time, remember? How often does a red-letter day like this come along?"

Hopefully never, since it implied having lived through another ghastly marriage. Laura had no intention of making that mistake again. The only man she wanted had a view on marriage that guaranteed he'd never repeat the experience, either.

With another merger successfully pulled off, Raoul left the Credit Suisse Banque and told the limo driver to take him to his apartment on the Boulevard General Guisan in Lausanne. He pealed off his suit jacket and tie. By the time he'd taken the private elevator to his penthouse overlooking Lake Geneva, he'd broken out in a cold sweat. It had soaked most of his shirt. He began unbuttoning it.

There was no point in lying to himself. He was in a depression nothing pulled him out of anymore. Since his marriage to Danielle had fallen apart, work had been his savior. Now not even another business transaction guaranteeing the Laroche Corporation would remain in the black for years to come brought him any pleasure. The realization that nothing seemed to matter disturbed him to a frightening level.

He needed a shower and a drink, not necessarily in that order. Tossing his clothes on the nearest chair, he headed for the liquor cabinet and almost stumbled over the pile of unread newspapers that had fallen out of the basket.

"*Bonsoir,* Raoul."

His head reared back before he came to a standstill.

Chantelle—

She was sitting in the middle of his couch looking better than he'd ever seen her, wearing an all-black cocktail dress with spaghetti straps. When she dressed for the kill, no one did it with more elegance. Her arms were outstretched on the back of the couch. She'd crossed her legs and was swinging one foot up and down, drawing his attention to her black high heels. She'd cut her hair in a short, becoming style that framed her face.

"Guy and Paul are meeting us here in fifteen minutes for dinner, so you and I don't have a lot of time."

"For what? I didn't invite you here."

She looked around. "The place is a mess. Marie told me you let her go until further notice. That didn't sound good." Her gaze came back to him. She stared without blinking. "Go ahead and get it off your chest. Tell me I'm the most evil, vile creature who ever climbed out from under a rock. Say it! 'You're less than a human being, Chantelle! You're not fit to breathe the same air as your husband and son!'

"I disagree of course. You can take it up with the Almighty when you get there. From the looks of the way your suit hangs on you, you're fading fast and it won't be long.

"One of your problems is, you never knew a love like mine and Guy's. He understood the second I told him. He forgave me because that's what real love is all about. After we made love, he admitted he would have done the same thing I did if our positions had been reversed. Remember something else. I never pushed our son away.

"Hearing that I was going to die—that I would be leaving Guy—was like a knife cutting the heart out of my body. It was either lie to him or ruin every day of his life sobbing in his arms. I could be much braver at a distance.

"I don't expect you to understand me. I don't expect you to like me, even if I adore you. What I do expect is that you come home. Of course, if there's a reason you can't because you're dying from some incurable disease you picked up rather recently and are too terrified to talk about, then who better than me to use for a sounding board. I've been there.

"Laura forgave me and wished me happiness.

Before she went back to California, she left me a letter with a box of my favorite truffles. It said that after seeing Guy and me together, she realized a great love like ours only comes along once in life and she understood why I tried to make my passing easier on my loved ones.

"I sent her a letter back telling her I forgave her for breaking her promise. I should have known she was so crazy in love with you she couldn't keep anything from you. Guy has always called her an angel. I believe she is. There's no guile in Laura. Beneath that gorgeous exterior, she's good clear through."

Raoul heard a sound behind him. When he jerked his head around, Guy was walking toward him with Paul. They'd never looked happier in their lives.

His nephew eyed him up and down. "I hate to say it Uncle Raoul, but *Maman* was right. You need help."

Guy smiled. "You do."

* * *

Laura put on some more sunscreen. She'd been sitting on the tower for the last hour. Four in the afternoon was the hottest time and the busiest. The last week of August was the best season of the year for tourists and locals to hit the beach.

From her perch she saw every sight imaginable. Lots of couples, some holding hands, others playing around throwing each other in the surf. Kids buried up to their necks in sand. Runners splashing in the water, teens playing volley ball. Life.

Her body gave a little heave of longing. To ward off the ache, she lifted the binoculars to her eyes. In her view she counted eighteen swimmers in the water. The surf was crumbly and didn't hang well. Not much wave to catch at the moment.

Five surfers eventually made their way back in on their boards and didn't go out again. Three kids on tubes moved further down the beach to the jurisdiction of the next lifeguard. Four guys in black wetsuits body surfed for ten minutes, then came in to play with a Frisbee. That left six people in the water. Two people wore life preservers. The other four were waiting to catch a big wave. They would have to be patient.

Finally one started to form way out. She could hear their shouts as they got ready to ride it. At first she counted four heads being swept in, coming closer, then there were three. The other swimmer had gotten pulled under. She waited for him to pop up again. When he did, she sensed he was in trouble. His head was back and his arms lifted in the air.

She removed her binoculars, jumped down from the tower and raced into the water at full speed, passing the other swimmers like a torpedo. If he'd taken in too much water, she'd have him back to shore and resuscitated before he suffocated.

When she was within five feet of him, he slid beneath the water. She immediately did a somersault that propelled her under him so she could get the hold on him to bring him up.

He was a strong, hard-muscled male with a

powerful physique, reminding her of Raoul. With his black hair, he could almost be the man whose memory had tortured her day and night.

When they broke water, she began the side crawl to bring him in, but he fought her. Sometimes a drowning victim panicked and didn't understand they needed to cooperate.

"Lie still and let me help you," she called out, but he struggled harder than anyone she'd ever saved. She feared she might not be able to do this alone. Frantic at this point, she kicked harder, trying to build momentum until he stopped resisting her. Hopefully someone on the beach realized what was happening and would bring help.

"Come on—let me do all the work," she cried in desperation. They were only halfway to shore now. Though it was a short distance, it seemed like miles. Then everything changed. Suddenly the man escaped her hold and she became his victim. With tremendous energy, he got her in the same grip she'd put on him and they headed full force for shore.

In the next breath he carried her to the beach and sank to his knees before laying her down. She felt his hands cup her face. She knew those hands and that body. Opening her eyes, she was met by a pair of piercing black ones.

"Raoul—"

"Don't talk, Laura," he whispered. "I'm about to give you the kiss of life. If you fight me, everyone on the beach will know it."

In her whole life, she'd never had to be saved, but if she *had* been drowning, her shock wouldn't have been as great as it was now.

He covered her mouth in an all-encompassing kiss that went on and on. For propriety's sake he couldn't touch her. His mouth had to make all the contact. Her senses responded, screaming for satisfaction only he could give.

When she didn't think she could stand it any longer if he didn't crush her beneath him, he relinquished her mouth with reluctance and sat back. "How are you feeling now?" he asked in a husky voice.

She was too dazed, and he was too gorgeous. A crowd had gathered round. She would have to tough her way out of this one.

Flashing everyone a smile, she rolled onto her side and got up, wiping the sand off her thighs. "Everything's under control," she told them. By now a leaner Raoul than she remembered had gotten to his feet, all six foot three of him. "Go on, everyone. Do what you were doing."

With smiles, the group dispersed little by little.

Raoul stared at her. "I for one intend to go on doing what I was doing with you. But not here. I arranged for another lifeguard to relieve you."

She looked over at the tower. Sure enough Mike Segal was there with a grin on his bronzed face. He waved and tossed her the beach bag that held all her essentials. Raoul caught it.

"My car's out in the parking lot by yours," he murmured. "Shall we leave yours here, or do you think you're recovered enough from your near drowning to drive and I'll follow you to your apartment."

She stared boldly at him. "It's the kiss of life that's made me so unstable."

"Let's go home and talk about it."

Laura started to tremble. "I don't want to talk. We always get in a fight."

His expression grew solemn. "I swear I won't let that happen."

"Raoul—" She couldn't take it again if they had words and he walked away.

"I came as soon as I could. You probably need your sandals." He handed her the bag.

She took it from him and pulled them out, but her gestures were all done in slow motion. This really wasn't happening. Raoul wasn't really here. She'd gotten too much sun and was hallucinating.

As she bent over, she reeled. He caught her against him and braced her body until she'd put them on. His lips brushed against her neck. "You feel so good I don't think I can walk, either."

"We have to!"

"Shall I carry you?"

"No!"

"We'll help each other."

Instead of two people who didn't like each other anymore, they put their arms around each other and slowly walked to the parking lot behind the palm trees bordering the sand.

He opened her car door and helped her in. "Please don't kiss me," she cried.

Without saying anything, he closed the door. She didn't mean it. The lazy smile he gave her let her know she didn't.

Still in a daze she watched him walk over to his rental car. He must have hidden the keys beneath the front mat. Still trembling, she rummaged for her keys and started the car.

Her apartment was only a mile and a half away. She pulled into her stall, then got out with her bag and signaled for him to park in the guest stall. With a suitcase in hand, he strode toward her. With every step her heart hammered harder.

He followed her inside the hallway. As soon

as she opened her door, she said, “Make yourself at home. You can have the shower first. The bathroom is the first door on the left down the hall past the living room.”

Afraid to look at him, she took off for the other part of the building. She needed time to absorb the fact that he’d flown to California to see her. After their last parting in his living room when she’d rushed toward Guy’s villa, she was positive she would never see him again.

Laura gave him ten minutes before she returned and found him in the living room on the couch, looking at one of her video game magazines. He’d dressed in tan trousers and a coffee-colored silk shirt. Everything he wore looked fabulous because he was such a striking man.

“I’ll be with you in a few minutes.”

He lifted his head and eyed her thoroughly. “Take your time. I’m not going anywhere.”

Laura showered in record time, then put on a pale-orange sundress with a little white jacket trimmed in orange plaid. She’d washed her hair.

After blow-drying it, she fastened it back in a French twist. Slipping into white sandals, she made her way to the kitchen.

"What can I get you?" she called to him.

"Water will do."

"One water coming up."

She grabbed two of them and walked into the other room. Afraid to get close to him, she placed his water on the coffee table before subsiding into one of the chairs opposite him.

Their eyes met. "You realize I'm never going to live this down with my colleagues."

He leaned forward to get his bottle. "It's past time someone did a favor for the lifeguard who has done at least five hundred saves by now."

"You read about that, too?" She unscrewed the lid of her bottle and took a long swig.

"Since Guy invited a Mrs. Aldridge into his home, I haven't been able to satisfy my curiosity enough about her."

"Is that why you're here?"

"No. I've come for an entirely different reason."

She pressed her lips together. "How's your family?"

He cocked his dark head. "Happier than I've seen them in years. Because of you, Guy and Chantelle are on a second honeymoon in Turkey with Paul."

Tears sprang to her eyes. "That's the best news I could ever hear. Though I realize what it has cost you to let me know, I thank you."

An odd sound came from his throat. "If you hadn't found the courage to force Chantelle to tell you why she was crying that day, we might all still be in the dark and suffering."

She swallowed hard. "You didn't feel that way about me the last time we were together. I realize that in keeping the truth from you about Chantelle as long as I did, it was the coup de grâce for you."

"My behavior was inhuman," he exclaimed in a voice of self-abnegation. "You have every right to tell me to get out and never come back. Why do you think I pretended to be drowning?

It was the only method I could think of that might give me the upper hand long enough to beg your forgiveness."

"That was very clever of you, but then I'd expect nothing less from Raoul Laroche. You make a powerful lifeguard yourself. Anytime you want a job, I'll put in a good word for you with my boss."

"What do I have to do to get in good with you?" The velvety question resonated to her bones. When she looked in his eyes, they looked suspiciously moist.

She fidgeted on the chair. "Since you continually find another reason to see me as the enemy, I don't know what to say. Do you realize we've never lasted more than a couple of hours without you throwing your darts at me?"

His expression grew bleak. "It began with Danielle. I've already told you a little about her, but not nearly enough. When I married her it was with the idea that we'd start a family right away. She *knew* how much I wanted to have children. After Paul was born, Chantelle couldn't conceive again because she went through early menopause."

"The poor thing," Laura moaned. "I've often wondered why they never had another baby when Paul is so wonderful. It's sad."

Raoul got to his feet with restless energy. "After two years of marriage without results we consulted Danielle's OB. He said to keep trying because he could find nothing wrong with either of us. If she didn't conceive within six months, he'd refer us to the fertility clinic.

"After four years I was ready to try in vitro, but Danielle fought me. At first I couldn't believe it. When I talked to Chantelle about it, she said she had the strongest suspicion my wife had been lying to me about wanting children.

"Once that seed was sown in my mind, I confronted Danielle. It was a nightmarish scene I wouldn't have an enemy live through. The moment she cowered from me, I *knew.* When she realized she was caught, it all came out.

She'd been on the pill long before our marriage took place and had never stopped taking them."

Laura shook her head. "Why?"

"She said we had the perfect marriage without children. She had friends whose marriages had failed because of children. Danielle didn't want that to happen to us."

A cry escaped Laura's throat. "I don't know how a woman could be that cruel. A lie like that would have turned me inside out, too, Raoul. I'm so sorry." It explained why he'd been so horrified over Chantelle's lie. "She had no right to do what she did."

"Danielle was too narcissistic to think beyond her own view of life."

"No wonder you lost your trust. Four years wasted when you could have divorced and married someone else who wanted children."

He rubbed the back of his neck absently. "At least when you went into your marriage, you and your husband both knew that you didn't want children."

Laura jumped out of the chair. "You're mistaken about that, Raoul," she cried. "I've always wanted children. Little Paulie made me want them more than ever. But soon after I married Ted, I fell out of love with him. There was no way I would bring a baby into a loveless marriage. It deserves the love of two parents who are madly in love with each other, like Chantelle and Guy."

Raoul looked stunned. "Is Ted still fighting your divorce?" he asked with new urgency.

"No. I won my divorce decree last week, August 15 to be exact."

A noticeable pallor appeared. "You mean you're free and clear of him?"

"Yes. I even had my name legally changed back to Aldridge. After Guy asked me if I would try to befriend Chantelle, it turned out to be an added blessing for me because Ted didn't know where I was.

"He broke into this apartment while I was away, and my friend Cindy across the hall documented it for me so I could take it to court. Because he ignored the restraining order and harassed me at my jobs, the judge granted the divorce without a problem." Her voice shook. "It was nice to know not everyone was in lockstep with the Stillmans."

"Laura—"

"Yes?" Her pulse was skidding off the charts.

"Do you want to have a baby with me?"

"Yes." She didn't have to think.

He blinked. "You just said yes."

She nodded. "I'm in love with you."

"That's what Chantelle said, but you couldn't be—"

"You mean after all the terrible things you've said and done to me?"

"I treated you so abominably, you have every right to throw me out."

"True, you have, but when you love someone the way I love you, you can forgive them anything."

"*When* did you know?" Now he was the one trembling.

"Well, it was lust at first sight in Guy's living room the night of his party and went downhill from there. I saw Mr. Adonis staring daggers at me. He was standing there with Maurice. I said to myself, 'I don't know how I'm going to do it, but I want to belong to that man forever.' And that was before I even knew if you were available or not."

He moved closer. His incredible black eyes were smiling. She'd only seen them do that a couple of times.

"It's your turn to tell me what I'm dying to hear." She smiled back at him. "But I'll let you off the hook. I don't think you can even say the words yet. It doesn't matter. I know what I feel. Anytime you want to get married, just tell me. I've been practicing writing my name in my sketchpad like all silly girls in love."

She walked over to the desk where it was lying and handed it to him. "Here. Take a look."

His breathing shallow, Raoul lifted the cover. She'd filled the first page with twenty lines of script. All said something different. "Madame

Raoul Laroche." "Madame Laurel Aldridge Laroche." "Monsieur et Madame Laroche." "Madelaine Laroche."

He darted her a glance. "Madelaine? That was my maternal grandmother's name."

"Chantelle told me. That's if we have a girl. If we have a boy first, then we need to think of something very special because he'll have such a special father."

Raoul put the pad down before pulling her into his arms. He rocked her for a long time. In his arms she felt she'd come home at last.

"I've been staying at my apartment in Switzerland since the day you flew here. Day before yesterday I walked in after work and realized that a life without you wasn't a life at all. I no longer cared if you didn't want children. As long as you loved me and only me, I'd deal with it.

"Make no mistake, Laura. I'm in love with you. You have to marry me soon. We're so good together."

"And so bad apart," she whispered against his lips before devouring them.

"You're so good." He ran his hands up and down her arms. "Guy saw the sweetness in you before he ever brought you into his home. The whole family loves you. I adore you." He kissed her fingertips.

"I love them." She slid her arms around his neck. "Kiss me, darling," her green eyes implored him. "Bring me back to life again."

Raoul needed no urging because she *was* his life.

MILLS & BOON PUBLISH EIGHT LARGE PRINT TITLES A MONTH. THESE ARE THE EIGHT TITLES FOR NOVEMBER 2009.

THE GREEK TYCOON'S BLACKMAILED MISTRESS
Lynne Graham

RUTHLESS BILLIONAIRE, FORBIDDEN BABY
Emma Darcy

CONSTANTINE'S DEFIANT MISTRESS
Sharon Kendrick

THE SHEIKH'S LOVE-CHILD
Kate Hewitt

THE BROODING FRENCHMAN'S PROPOSAL
Rebecca Winters

HIS L.A. CINDERELLA
Trish Wylie

DATING THE REBEL TYCOON
Ally Blake

HER BABY WISH
Patricia Thayer